THE FIFTH RECKONING

Hunter Critt

Published by Blister House Press

ISBN: 979-8-218-90065-6

Cover design by Fosley Design Art

Printed in the United States of America

First Edition

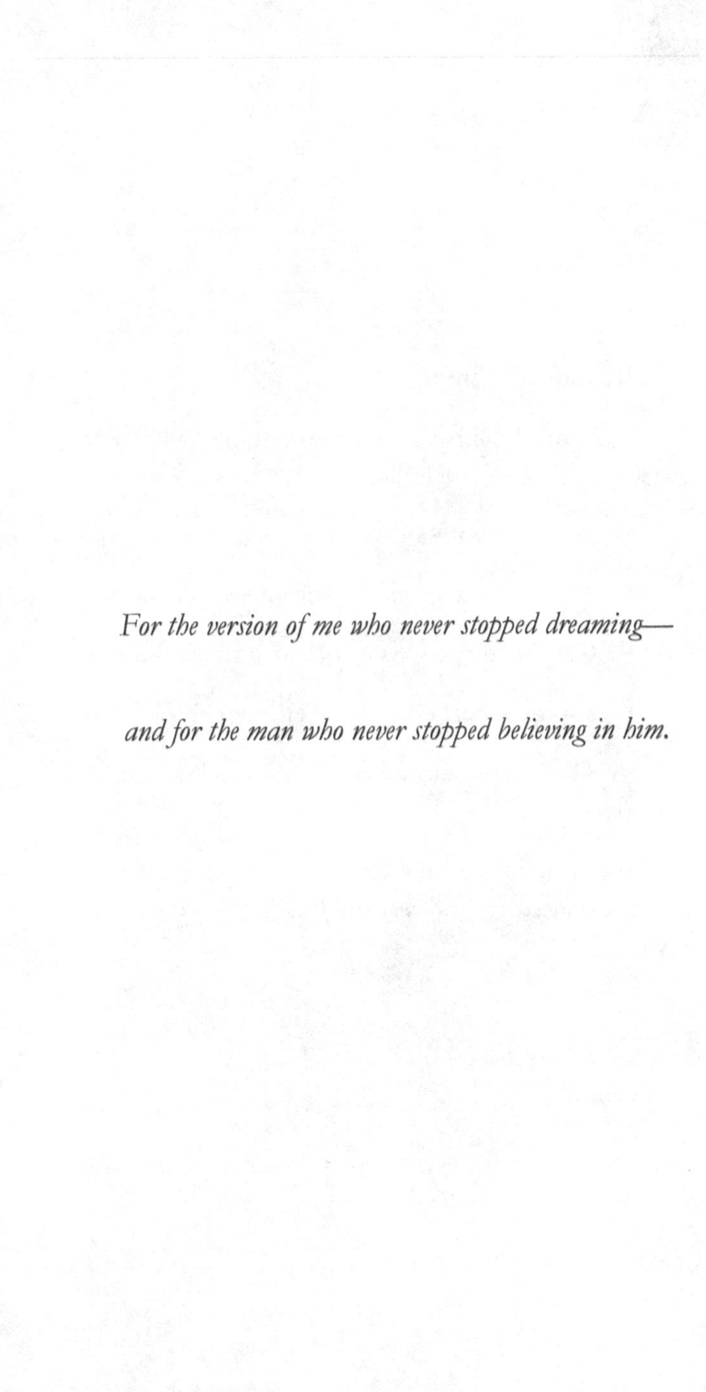

For the version of me who never stopped dreaming—

and for the man who never stopped believing in him.

Reader Advisory

This novel contains mature and potentially distressing content, including:

- Parental death and grief

- Abduction and home invasion

- Graphic depictions of blood, gore, and murder

- Psychological horror and emotional trauma

- Themes of betrayal, isolation, and internal struggle

While fictional, these elements are portrayed with emotional intensity and realism. Reader discretion is advised.

Acknowledgements:

Finishing this book has been a dream long in the making, and I wouldn't have reached this moment without the quiet persistence and support of those around me.

To my husband—thank you for your unwavering belief, your patience, and your love. You held space for this story when I couldn't, and your strength carried me through every doubt.

To Megan—your insight, continuity checks, and creative feedback helped shape this book in ways that readers may never see, but I'll never forget. Your support behind the scenes made the writing stronger and the process lighter.

To my beta readers—thank you for your time, honesty, and encouragement. Your early eyes helped refine the rough edges and gave me the confidence to move forward. This story is sharper, deeper, and more complete because of you.

To every reader who finds themselves in these pages—thank you for trusting me with your time and attention. I wrote this story for the ones who've felt alone, betrayed, or broken. May you find something here that reminds you you're not.

And finally, to myself—thank you for not giving up. For showing up, page after page, even when it felt impossible. This book is proof that the dream was worth chasing.

Prologue

It began twenty-five years ago—with a message no one could stop, and a threat no one could understand. A mass video was sent out, hijacking every screen on Earth. For one breathless moment, the world froze. Time itself seemed to stop. A breath of silence, the calm before the storm. The warning that the entire human race needed to heed for the sake of the world.

"Good evening, we regret to inform you that the entire human race is now in the hands of eight individuals." A terrifying mask filled the screen—dark, metallic, with tusks like a wild boar, but sharper, dripping with something that looked like oil or blood. Steam hissed from the mask in tendrils, coiling around the figure like serpents.

The screens began to flash photos of the eight people who had been abducted from their homes and jobs. These people would become the Selected. *"These individuals will compete in a series of trials. They will be televised from beginning to end. So long as one survivor makes it out of the trials alive, humanity will be spared. If they fail, you all shall perish."*

The video ends with a clip of a large laser that wipes out an entire line of trees in a forest. Ash blanketed the forest floor. Not a single limb remained. The trees were erased. This kind of weaponry was beyond what any country in the world was capable of, at least that was what we had all been told. A terrifying figure stood at the edge of the tree line, dressed in a black cloak, holding a scythe with blood dripping from the curved blade. A euphemism of death and destruction. A promise of what would come if the Selected failed.

World leaders met from around the globe, pointing fingers at one another and trying to determine which country was powerful enough to pull this off. Leaders concluded that the force was unknown and external. This caused a pandemonium of chaos around the globe. Stores were ransacked; businesses reduced to ash as people tried to gather supplies to barricade themselves in their homes.

A crackdown on military and police protocol restored order after weeks of discord. A treaty was formed. No wars would be waged until we find and eliminate this threat. An illusion of world peace.

Across the globe this unnamed entity streamed the suffering—bones breaking, screams echoing, minds unraveling. The trials weren't just physical. They were also psychological in nature. Breaking the "contestants" and bringing terror to the world. They were engineered to destroy.

Each trial escalated in cruelty, designed to break the body, then the mind. Finally, after two brutal months of waiting, the trials end. One person has survived by the skin of his teeth. It appears that this individual has been let go and has returned to his normal life. As normal as one can be when subjected to the psychological terrors that were endured. Then the government officials swarm in and take him into custody, trying to get as much information from him as they can. No new leads are offered up and the victor of the trials is never heard from again.

Everyone seemed to breathe a sigh of relief once the trials ended, no further contact was made. After years of peace, the world seemed to return to normal. The trials all but forgotten. A dark smudge on history that the world was trying to erase. The peace treaty was dropped, and world leaders were back to their regularly scheduled destruction.

But peace was only temporary. Five years later, the Mask returned. The same disturbing message. The same demented protocol. Eight more lives were stolen into their secret gaming center. The peace treaty was reinstated as governments pooled resources to locate the facility—but no trace was ever found.

The trials continued every five years. One survivor each time, broken and hollow. Questioned. Forgotten. Twenty-five years ago, it began. Now, the fifth reckoning begins. And this time, the game master isn't just watching—he's choosing.

1.

Escape Room

"A little help in here" she said facing the camera. "We are going to *die* if you don't help us."

"Don't be dramatic. Here is a hint," Rueben said.

Rueben Bentley rolled his eyes; they always said the same thing. As if dying in a simulation made it real. He grabbed the sheet of paper that had the clues laid out in order. He was the game master for the hardest escape room in Velbridge. Ever since the first invasion, escape rooms have become more than entertainment. They were rehearsal spaces for panic, logic, and the illusion of control. A way to adapt and survive this brutal new reality.

"I love to have a cup of tea, even when I feel down in the dumps," he said over the intercom. One of the players in the room screamed as he finished his sentence, ran to the bistro table, and flipped it upside down. The metal legs bent slightly as if about to break, the loud screech of metal echoing out of the security feed making Rueben wince.

"Try not to break anything," he groaned over the intercom.

On the bottom of the table was a laminated piece of white paper with numbers typed out in boldface. It was the combination of the safe on the opposite side of the room.

Rueben had taken over designing most of the games after he was hired at *EscapeMeNot*. His puzzles were brutal, elegant, and just survivable enough to keep people coming back. After impressing the company that quietly funded the operation—never named, but always watching—he was promoted to creative director.

Now, players fly in from all over the world to assess themselves against their rooms. They weren't deadly, not officially. But Rueben understood the appeal. Every clue solved felt like proof you might survive the next incursion. Every locked door was a rehearsal for the real thing.

This year marked the twenty-fifth anniversary of the first Trials. Every five years, eight people were taken—no warning, no pattern—and forced to play for their lives, and for the fate of humanity.

The Trials were supposed to begin three days ago. But no videos had surfaced. No one had been reported missing.

People were scared. Streets emptied well before night fall. Homes were boarded up, as if plywood could stop what was coming.

The Masked Ones—what the figures in the leaked videos were called now—had proven, year after year, that nowhere was safe. One year, they pulled someone from an underground bunker. Another, from a high-security prison cell. No alarms. No witnesses. Just a new video, a new set of players, and the dread that came with it.

Rueben's escape room had just the one group scheduled today. Smaller than usual. Others were too nervous. He couldn't blame them. Everyone was waiting for the Trials to begin. And this year, the silence felt worse than the spectacle.

The quiet dread didn't touch Rueben much. There were billions of people. The odds of being one of the Selected were slim.

"OMG, OMG, WE DID IT!"

The girl's voice tore through the intercom, yanking Rueben out of his thoughts.

He sighed and stepped into the hallway, passing eight rows of identical doors—each one a portal to panic, puzzles, and pretend survival.

The group spilled out of the room, all four girls around his age, flushed with adrenaline and self-congratulation.

The dramatic one—loud, theatrical, and convinced she'd cracked the most riddles—was practically vibrating with pride. Rueben gave her a polite nod, already tuning out the noise.

"You'd probably still die if you were one of the Selected," one of her friends muttered, shutting the door behind her.

"Hey now, no need for bullying," Rueben said, handing them the victory sign from the closet. "You solved a brutal puzzle. Gloating is earned. Only three groups have beaten this room since it launched last month."

He watched them celebrate, already thinking about the next game. The one he planned to pitch to management in the morning. It would be the hardest yet—puzzles designed to push players past their limits.

The team had agreed: the rooms needed to be tougher. More realistic. The innovative design required a signed waiver. Not for show. There was a real chance someone could get hurt. Maybe worse.

But in order to start designing the room, they needed permission from the city.

Rueben had led the charge in court, arguing that the room would serve the public good. That it would prepare people for the Trials. The city had hesitated—after all, the odds of being Selected were slim. But Rueben could be persuasive. Especially when survival was on the line.

The courtroom smelled like old paper and polished wood. Rueben stood at the podium, sleeves rolled up, tie loosened—not out of disrespect, but defiance.

"Let me be clear," he said, voice steady. "This isn't entertainment. It's preparation."

A murmur rippled through the chamber. The city's legal counsel, a woman with steel-gray hair and a stack of objections, leaned forward. "You're asking us to approve an 'escape room' where participants could die. Voluntarily."

"Yes," Rueben said. "Because the Trials won't ask permission."

He tapped the waiver packet on the podium. "Every participant signs the waiver, and every participant must be of legal age. Every puzzle is vetted. But the point isn't safety—it's survival. Do you want citizens who freeze when the Selection comes? Or ones who've already faced the edge and learned how to take back their independence? This game could vastly increase humanities shot at survival. There could be more than one survivor."

The judge raised an eyebrow. "And you believe this room will help?"

Rueben didn't blink. "I know it will."

Behind him, the company's legal team shifted uneasily. They'd warned him to soften the pitch. To emphasize community, resilience, bonding. But Rueben knew the truth wouldn't sell itself.

"We've run simulations. We've tracked behavioral shifts. The rooms work. They strip away comfort and reveal instinct. That's what the Trials demand. The Masked has yet to be caught. I am offering a way to fight back."

The judge glanced at the city rep. "And the death clause?"

Rueben leaned in. "It's not a clause. It's a possibility. Just like the real world. It is no different than crossing the street or getting in your car. Every decision you make could be your last."

Silence. Then the gavel struck.

"Motion approved. Proceed with caution."

Those words still echoed in Rueben's head as he sat behind the front desk, the hum of the building barely masking the unease outside.

The city felt different now. Tighter. Like something was coiling beneath the surface.

He had posted the victory photo minutes ago—four girls grinning, unaware of how close they'd come to running out of time. Rueben had smiled at them, handed them the sign, even congratulated their teamwork. But his mind had been elsewhere.

The pitch folder lay open beside him, filled with sketches and fragments of memory.

This new room wouldn't just be difficult. It would be a mirror.

Rueben tapped his pen against the desk, eyes drifting over the blueprint. The puzzles would mimic the Trials—not the sanitized versions people whispered about, but the real ones. The ones that had shaped him.

He had been five when the first victims were taken.

Too young to understand, too curious to obey.

His parents had tried to shield him from the broadcasts, but the Trials were everywhere. Every screen in the house was transmitting the terror.

Rueben used to sit at the top of the stairs, peering through the railing while the footage played on their television below. The contestants moved like prey—hesitant, desperate, calculating.

He remembered the silence before the first scream.

That was when he learned: survival wasn't about strength. It was about instinct.

And instinct could be taught.

As bad as it sounded, he used to look forward to the next wave of tests.

Work stopped. School paused. The city held its breath.

And Rueben? He read. He sketched puzzles. He watched strangers die on screen and felt… curious. Detached. It was like a horror movie, but this one was unscripted.

He didn't know those people.

But he knew the patterns.

The new room would mimic those patterns.

Not to glorify them.

To prepare people for what was coming.

Rueben blinked, pulled back to the present by the sharp screech of sirens outside the store.

Rueben stayed at the desk long after the four girls had left, staring at the pitch folder like it might rearrange itself into something less brutal.

But the city wouldn't wait. And neither would the Trials.

He locked up for the night, slipping the folder into his bag.

The walk to work that morning had been normal—almost cheerful. Pedestrians chatting, buses rumbling, cars honking in impatience. The city had still felt alive.

The walk home was a different story.

Rueben passed shuttered windows and darkened porches. Most homes had gone quiet, lights off, curtains drawn. A couple walked their dog in silence. A college-aged runner jogged past with earbuds in, eyes scanning the shadows.

No cars. No chatter. Just Rueben and the sound of his own footsteps echoing back off the silent houses.

The city was bracing for something.

And Rueben was already planning how to simulate it.

It wasn't until Rueben rounded the corner to his house that he understood why the streets had emptied.

Far off in the distance, hovering above the rooftops, was a ship.

Massive. Silent. Triangular—like a mountain suspended in the sky.

Its surface gleamed silver, catching the last light of the sun and scattering it across the quiet neighborhood. It hummed softly, a low vibration that seemed to settle in Rueben's bones.

How had he not seen it before?

His stomach churned.

Then came the flash.

A burst of blue light cracked across the sky, followed by a sizzling wave of electricity that made his hair stand on end. The air itself felt charged, like the moment before a lightning strike.

And just like that, the dread settled in.

It had begun.

The Selected were being chosen.

2.

The Chamber

His breath caught. The barking of a dog echoed like gunfire, distant but sharp. He blinked, once, twice—then bolted. He was fumbling with his keys trying to get into the house but could not find the key that turned the lock. He had car keys, house keys, and work keys all on the same keyring and now he was regretting it.

This was not the first time that the invasions had taken place, but this was the only time that they had been so close to home. On screen, the ships were cinematic—distant, stylized, unreal. But this one hovered above his hometown like a verdict. It wasn't being broadcast anymore. It was a sentence. This no longer felt like a movie on television, and more like he had just stepped into one of his very own escape rooms.

They'd started big—Tokyo. High-rises, nightclubs, even crowded intersections. The Masked didn't just arrive; they performed.

The winner that year was a neurosurgeon. Ninety-six percent success rate. After the trials, he vanished. The government said he was insisting that he was "under protection" in case the Masked returned for him. No one believed them.

Rueben walked through the house and began silently preparing his hideout. While most of the time he seemed like he did not care about the invasions, he wasn't an idiot. He was prepared just like everyone else was. Even if the preparations were just for comfort.

Tomorrow would likely be a day off—courtesy of the impending takeover. He told himself that the extra day off meant more time to polish his escape room pitch. But the truth was, he'd spend most of it pacing, checking feeds, and pretending the world wasn't unraveling.

He walked to the back of the house, stopping every few feet to peer out the window at the ship in the sky. Was it getting closer? He couldn't see the ship well from inside and it was making him nervous.

He entered his room and walked straight to the bookshelf on the left side of his bed. He grabbed the copy of *War of the Worlds* and tilted it back off the shelf, unlocking the secret doorway. War of the Worlds. A little

on the nose, maybe. But Rueben liked the symbolism—
fiction unlocking reality.

The metal door shut behind him, sealing him off
from the world. The air inside was cooler and drier. He
reached to his right and hit the switch. Lights started to
flicker on in front of him one by one. A slim hallway
illuminating before him, slanting down toward a spiral
staircase. The hum of the lights echoed like a distant
engine. The black metal stairs led to the main entrance of
the bunker. The room opened into a large space with two
velvety green couches facing a wall of televisions. A small
kitchenette was off to the left corner that led to a fully
stocked pantry with cases of water and non-perishable
foods. To the right behind the staircase was a small
bathroom with a shower that you might find on a cruise
ship. Rueben had built the bunker after inheriting the
house. The basement felt too exposed, too ordinary.

He just hoped that the Masked was not targeting
him, since other bunkers had proved to be useless in
protecting anyone from the invaders. His bunker was
more for fallout from any impending battle that would
take place once the government figured out how to fight
back. The first invasion had been met with fighter jets
and military personnel. The ship proved to be
impenetrable, and the defenses were deemed worthy of
any opposing force. The fight was over shortly after it
had begun, dozens of lives lost. The Masked took out all
the bombers in quick succession and then disappeared in
the cloud of dust.

Being down here now felt less like survival and more like surrender. Like he'd sealed himself off from the world just in time to watch it end.

Rueben sank into one of the velvety green couches, the silence pressing in around him. He figured he had a few hours—at best—before every screen on Earth was hijacked.

He reached in the side table, pulled out his laptop, and wirelessly connected it to the wall of televisions.

One file. One obsession.

The Trials began to play.

Rueben had watched them countless times, dissecting every movement, every scream, every puzzle. He wanted to get it right. To build something that could help people survive if they were ever chosen.

But tonight, something felt different.

The footage flickered across the screen—faces twisted in fear, bodies collapsing, choices made too late.

Rueben felt it then. Remorse.

He was rewatching death. Repackaging it into a fun-filled evening for teenagers.

He swallowed hard.

This is for the greater good, he told himself. You're doing what others won't. You're pushing the boundaries.

If you watch this again, you can help someone survive.

He repeated it like a prayer.

But the guilt didn't leave.

The video playing now was one of the more disturbing trials.

Five players had made it this far—fourth or fifth trial, Rueben couldn't be sure anymore. Some of them bled into each other, back-to-back, like a fever dream.

The room was cavernous. Pillars stretched from floor to ceiling, casting long, skeletal shadows across the walls. In the center stood a metal wheel—massive, rusted, and cruelly designed.

Four triangles were etched into its surface, evenly spaced and just large enough to hold a body. It looked like a knife-throwing wheel, the kind used in circus acts or twisted game shows. But this wasn't for entertainment.

Belt-like cuffs hung from each triangle, stiff with dried blood. The buckles rusted, giving off a sick glow from the low light.

Rueben leaned forward, eyes locked on the screen.

He'd seen this trial before.

And yet, every time, it felt worse.

The players shuffled toward the wheel, hesitant, scanning the room for any sign of danger. Their eyes darted between the pillars, the shadows, the ceiling— anywhere a threat might emerge.

Every footstep echoed, loud and unforgiving, amplifying the tension as they tried to stay quiet. The silence stretched, taut and suffocating.

Then—

A metallic scrape shattered the stillness.

Shadows sprang to life, dancing across the walls. The players recoiled, backing into one another as hooded figures darted between the pillars, their cackles rising from the darkest corners.

The swarm descended.

They fought back, but it was futile. The Masked were too strong, too fast. One by one, the players were slammed against the wheel, their limbs strapped into blood-stained cuffs.

One player remained untouched.

Spared—or chosen.

A whirring sound cut through the chaos.

A panel rose from the floor, sleek and cold, equipped with four buttons. Each one pulsed faintly, waiting.

Rueben didn't blink.

The wheel spun, groaning like it was alive. Blood streaked across the metal, dripping in slow arcs as the players thrashed against their restraints.

He leaned forward, elbows on knees, eyes locked on the one in front of the panel.

Would I panic?

The thought came uninvited.

Would I scream? Would I beg? Or would I freeze, calculating odds while someone else bled out?

The speaker crackled.

"ALAN, YOU HAVE BEEN SELECTED…"

Rueben reached for his sketchpad.

His own wheel design was cleaner. Sleek. Sterile. No blood. No screams. Just theory.

He flipped to the page labeled Trial Mechanics: Sacrifice Logic.

Four buttons. Four lives. One choice.

He drew the panel again, this time annotating each button with possibilities:

- Button A: Immediate "death"

- Button B: Delayed release

- Button C: Randomized outcome

- Button D: False hope

He circled "False hope" twice.

That's the cruelest one, he thought. The one that makes you believe you did the right thing.

The panel in the real trials were each designed to save a specific player, but Rueben wanted to change his game just enough to be original. Enough to not feel like a reenactment.

Rueben rewound the footage. Alan's hand hovered. Trembled.

Rueben sketched the wheel's rotation again—counterclockwise, slow, deliberate.

He scribbled notes:

- Blood flow increases tension

- Groaning sound = psychological trigger

- Button delay = forced hesitation

His pen paused.

This isn't just a game. It's a test of empathy under duress.

He stared at Alan.

Choose wisely, the voice said.

Rueben whispered it to himself.

"Choose wisely."

Rueben's breath caught as the wheel groaned, tilting the girl upside down. Her face flushed crimson, tears streaking toward the floor.

The floor beneath the wheel slid open revealing a pit of spikes underneath.

Stepping forward, one of the Masked pulled out an apple.

He tossed the apple on the spikes, impaling it.

He pointed at Alan and motioned to the panel.

The spikes below gleamed. The apple dripping as it slid further down the sharp metal.

Rueben felt it—a pang, sharp and sudden.

She's real.

He blinked hard, then reached for his sketchpad.

The page was already half-filled with diagrams. He flipped to a fresh sheet, drew the wheel again, this time with the pit beneath it.

Spikes = visual threat. Apple = psychological trigger.

He annotated quickly:

- Rotation speed: slow enough to prolong panic

- Blood rush = disorientation

- Upside-down position = vulnerability amplification

He paused.

Would I pass out? Would I scream?

He hated that he didn't know.

Rueben rewound the footage, watching the girl's breathing, the way her fingers twitched against the restraints. She was grasping for anything to keep herself from sliding out into the pit below. Blood oozing from her wrists making it harder for her to get a good grip.

Her eyes were fluttering and her breaths were ragged as she slipped under, eyes closing like she was meditating.

He circled her in the sketch.

Survivability window: 90 seconds before unconsciousness?

His pen hovered.

This isn't just cruelty. It's timing.

He flipped back to his own wheel design. It was too clean. Too theoretical.

Rueben began to redraw it—adding the pit, the spikes, the rotation mechanism.

But he hesitated.

Do I really want to replicate this?

The laughter of the Masked echoed from the speakers. Rueben flinched.

He scribbled a note at the bottom of the page:

Design for survival, not spectacle.

Then, almost as an afterthought:

She was real.

He rewound the video again.

"Alan, Please, I have three kids waiting for me at home," she pleads.

"I have to take care of my mother," says the younger man who is now at the top of the wheel.

Voices erupt as all the players start talking in unison trying to persuade Alan to make the right decision.

"This is difficult. I don't know what to do." Alan was choking back a sob as he looked over all of them.

The players all plead and beg as Alan stands there with his hands hovering over the buttons. Each pass of the wheel makes the players increasingly uneasy. The girl passed out from spinning for so long.

"MAKE A DECISION SOON OR YOU ALL SHALL PERISH," was heard echoing through the room.

Alan is now closer to the panel. He is crying and shaking. You can see the turmoil running through his mind. His hand briefly hovers over each of the buttons as he tries to make this life altering decision. Rueben is not sure how the Masked can just stand there and allow these trials to take place. Rueben would fight back if he was in their position, find a way out. Alan finally reaches toward the panel, seeming to have decided. At the very last minute he lunges past the panel.

Rueben's breath caught.

Alan dove.

Not toward a door. Not toward survival.

Toward the spikes.

The room on screen erupted—hooded figures shrieking, the wheel grinding to a halt, the remaining players frozen in disbelief.

Rueben stared, unmoving.

His sketchpad lay open beside him, half-filled with notes on button logic and sacrifice mechanics.

None of it mattered now.

Alan had broken the system.

Rueben rewound the footage, watching the moment again. The hesitation. The trembling hand. The final lunge.

He chose no one. He chose himself.

Rueben scribbled a single line beneath his diagram:

What happens when the player refuses to play?

He sat back, the bunker suddenly feeling smaller.

The Masked had designed a trial to force cruelty. Alan had answered with sacrifice.

Rueben did not know whether to admire him or mourn him.

He closed the sketchpad.

For the first time in hours, he did not press play.

It just kept replaying in his head.

Alan's body—gone.

The woman's scream—still echoing.

Rueben had not moved from his seat. The footage looped again, and again, and again in his head. Blood. Screams. Silence.

Finally, he pressed play again to watch what the end of the trial. He needed to study the reactions.

The Masked moved like clockwork, cutting the players down with surgical precision. No words. No comfort. Just the hiss of hydraulics as the door swung open.

The survivors did not speak. They stumbled forward, dazed, like cattle released from a pen. One of them looked back—just once—before the door sealed behind them.

Rueben paused the video.

His fingers hovered over the pen, but he couldn't pick it up. Not yet.

Alan's choice had broken something. Not the trial. Not the system.

Rueben.

He leaned back, eyes scanning the ceiling of the bunker, as if expecting answers to be etched into the concrete.

What kind of man builds a game that ends like this?

He didn't know anymore.

He watched again as the door slammed shut with a bang.

He froze.

The bang was not part of the trial. It wasn't on the screen.

It was above him.

Rueben's heart sank into his stomach, cold and heavy. The bunker had always felt safe—sealed, reinforced, buried beneath layers of concrete and paranoia. But now, someone was trying to get in.

He muted the video. The silence was worse.

Another thud. Louder. Closer.

The ceiling groaned.

Dust trickled down from the seam near the ventilation shaft.

They found me.

He backed toward the wall, eyes darting to the spiral stairs.

Could he make it up and out in time? Probably not.

Rueben's mind raced—not with escape plans, but with questions.

Was this about the trials? Had someone seen what he'd built?

He thought of Alan. Of the blood. Of the scream.

Another bang. This time, louder.

He wasn't ready to die.

But he wasn't ready to face what he'd created either.

3.

Abduction

Fear gripped Rueben like a vice.

The Masked were trying to break into his home—his haven, his safety net.

He fumbled with the remote, hands trembling as he stabbed at the input button. The screens flickered, then shifted to show the interior camera feeds. Hallways. Entry points. Shadows.

He'd installed the system after the fourth invasion, right after inheriting the house. It had felt like the only rational thing to do.

His eyes flicked to the family photo on the table beside him. He sighed.

They had always hidden in the basement.

Rueben never trusted the basement. Too exposed. Too obvious. That's why he built the bunker—reinforced steel, hidden access, layered security. It was supposed to be enough.

But it never really was.

He'd read the reports. Seen the footage. People taken from bunkers, panic rooms, and underground vaults. Precautions didn't matter when the Masked wanted you.

And still, the dread lingered—not just from the invasion, but from what had happened in this house.

Switching from camera to camera, Rueben finally found the source of the noise.

The Masked were at his front door.

They rammed it again—this time with what looked like a metal ram's head—splintering the frame in a violent burst. Fragments of wood shot across the living room, piercing the couch, shattering trinkets. Only a sliver of the door remained on its hinge, swinging like a broken limb.

Rueben's stomach dropped.

The Masked were inside, tearing through drawers, tossing furniture, rifling through shelves. They weren't just searching—they were hunting.

He began to pace, silently, mechanically. His thoughts scrambled. This town was massive. He'd convinced himself they wouldn't bother with him. That he was just another face in the crowd.

Why me?

A crash snapped his attention back to the screens.

The kitchen.

Glasses shattered. Plates flew. Silverware scattered like shrapnel.

Rueben's fear twisted into fury.

How could I be hiding among the dishes? This wasn't tactical—it was theatrical. A power move. A message.

The Masked weren't just invading.

They were performing.

And Rueben was their audience.

Rueben paced again, his thoughts spiraling.

If he'd been upstairs, maybe he could've fought back. The bat behind his bedroom door—how many could he have taken out before they overwhelmed him? The butcher's knife on the counter—he smirked at the thought of slicing through one of their hands for smashing his things. The machete in the garage, hanging among his tools—just off the kitchen. He could've made it there. Maybe.

But it was all fantasy.

Rueben stopped pacing.

The truth settled in, heavy and cold.

He was scared. He had always been scared.

He wore nonchalance like armor, treating the Trials like background noise—just another grim fact of life, like war or famine. Something you saw on the news, talked about over dinner, but never really felt.

Until it came for you.

Rueben stopped pacing.

The screens showed the kitchen in ruins—glass glittering across the tile, silverware scattered like bones. One of the Masked kicked open the pantry door, then slammed it shut when they found nothing inside.

They weren't just searching.

They were escalating.

Rueben's eyes flicked to the hallway feed. Another figure had entered. Taller. Slower. Deliberate.

This one wasn't rifling through drawers.

It was looking at the walls.

At the photos.

At the family.

Rueben's breath caught.

He stepped closer to the screen, heart thudding.

The figure reached out, touched the frame of the photo on the mantle. The one with Rueben as a child. The one with his mother.

Then it turned—slowly—and stared directly into the camera.

Rueben stumbled back.

They know.

Rueben was still reeling when he noticed the silence.

Too quiet.

He glanced at the screen. The kitchen was empty. No movement. No destruction. Just shards of glass and overturned chairs.

A flicker of relief passed through him.

Maybe they gave up. Maybe they thought I wasn't home. Maybe they'll go after someone else.

The thought made him wince. He didn't want anyone else to feel this kind of fear.

He flipped through the remaining camera feeds.

His stomach dropped.

They hadn't left.

They were in his bedroom.

This was no longer random. This was personal.

His room was sacred—his sanctuary. Every detail had been chosen with care. The huge bay window on the left flooded the space with natural light. Houseplants hung from the ceiling and clustered across the floor, a living tapestry of green. Nestled among them was his velvet chaise lounge, perfectly positioned for reading.

His bed sat at the center—memory foam, soft velvet duvet, a cocoon of comfort. On either side, tall bookshelves framed the space, with sconce lights casting a warm glow. The headboard was fitted with outlets, a quiet nod to practicality.

It was the one place he felt safe.

His mind flashed back to the wreckage in the kitchen, heat rising in his cheeks.

Now, the Masked stood in his bedroom.

They weren't moving.

It looked like they were speaking to one another, but Rueben didn't dare turn on the sound. If they heard the TV, it was over.

Three figures.

Two were tall—six feet, broad shoulders, masks shaped like devils. Horns curled back, sharp, and symmetrical, like something carved from bone.

The third was smaller. Rueben's height. But his presence was heavier.

His mask was black, tusked, and terrifying. Twin ivory blades jutted from the sides of the jaw, and horns crowned the top like a twisted halo. In the grayscale feed, the teeth gleamed unnaturally white. The horns were shaded—Rueben could only assume they were red.

He stared at the screen, pulse pounding.

They weren't just invading.

They were inspecting.

The three figures began to move—slowly, methodically—scanning every inch of the room.

Rueben's heart sank.

Just to the left of the bed, near the edge of the bookshelf, a small piece of purple fabric lay on the floor.

He glanced down at his shirt.

The bottom hem was torn.

His palms began to sweat. His chest tightened. He couldn't breathe.

Seconds dragged like hours as he watched the Masked comb through his sanctuary. The smaller figure noticed it first—tilting its head, then motioning to the others. They gathered around the fabric, staring at the bookshelf.

One of the larger brutes gripped the shelf's edge and yanked, but it didn't budge. He slumped in disappointment.

Then the smaller one leaned in, scanning the titles.

Rueben's breath hitched.

The figure's finger traced each spine, slow and deliberate. Then it paused.

Its shoulders began to shake.

It was laughing.

Rueben could feel it—mocking him.

The finger tilted a book back.

The door slid open.

Rueben doesn't have any time at all to think. He can hear the footsteps at the top of the stairs, and he knows they are coming to the end of the hallway. There is a slight shuffling sound and some faint whispering. He is panicking now. He can't breath and is starting to feel lightheaded.

Rueben didn't have time to think.

The footsteps above grew louder, more deliberate. He could hear them reaching the end of the hallway— then a pause. Shuffling. Whispering. The kind that made his skin crawl.

His breath came in short, ragged bursts. His chest felt tight, like the air had thickened around him. He was lightheaded, dizzy, and the room felt smaller by the second.

Then came the sound.

Metal on metal.

A soft clink, followed by a hollow bounce. Rueben turned toward the stairs just in time to see it—a small, round object tumbling down, catching the light as it clanged against each step.

It sounded impossibly loud.

A grenade?

His body moved before his mind could catch up. He ducked behind the couch, heart hammering, limbs trembling. But then the realization hit him like a second explosion.

They weren't here to kill him.

They needed him alive.

This wasn't shrapnel—it was smoke.

Rueben scrambled to the kitchenette, nearly slipping on the tile. He yanked open the drawer, grabbed a washcloth, and shoved it under the faucet. The water was cold, almost shocking. He wrung it out with shaking hands, pressed it to his mouth, and took three deep breaths—trying to fill his lungs with clean air before the inevitable.

The hiss came next.

A sharp, pressurized burst.

Then the smoke.

It poured into the room like a living thing—green, thick, and fast. It curled around the furniture, swallowed the walls, and coated the air with a strange, floral sweetness.

Lavender.

Rueben gagged. His lungs burned. His mouth watered uncontrollably. The cloth helped, but not enough. The smoke was everywhere—dense, invasive, clinging to his skin like static.

He dropped to the floor, crawling toward the far wall, trying to stay low. His eyes stung. His vision blurred. The room spun like a carousel.

They scented it on purpose, he thought. A final kindness before unconsciousness? Or just another layer of control?

He could barely see the screens now. Just flickers of light through the haze.

The vents kicked in—finally. A low hum filled the room as the air began to shift, pulling the smoke upward. He'd designed them for this exact scenario. He'd tested them. Measured airflow. Calculated dispersal rates.

But now, watching the smoke crawl toward him like a predator, it felt like a child's solution to a monster's problem.

His knees buckled.

He gripped the edge of the counter, trying to stay upright, trying to stay awake.

But the lavender was everywhere.

And Rueben was fading.

He could hear the footsteps descending the stairs.

This was it.

Rueben had to decide—now.

He scanned the room. Empty. Bare. No weapons. How had he forgotten? Maybe it was the rush, the panic when he first dove into the bunker. He'd thought he had more time.

He dropped on the floor.

Maybe he could run. Maybe if he played unconscious, the shock of him springing up would buy him a few seconds—just enough to escape.

The footsteps grew louder. Closer.

He lay still, chest rising too fast, vision swimming from the gas. His limbs felt heavy. His thoughts were slipping.

FIGHT IT, RUEBEN. THIS IS YOUR ONLY CHANCE.

Then—contact.

A strong hand gripped his shoulder.

Adrenaline surged.

Rueben shot up, shoving the figure backward with everything he had. It was the shorter one—the tusked Masked. He stumbled, crashing into his brute of a companion with a guttural shout.

Rueben didn't wait.

He was already moving—legs pumping, lungs burning, vision blurred but focused on the stairs.

He didn't look back.

Rueben ran, legs pumping, lungs burning. The short distance to the stairs vanished beneath him.

He grabbed the railing, pulling hard, trying to take two steps at a time—anything to gain speed, to get away.

Just as he lifted his leg—

A hand shot out.

Cold. Strong. Final.

It clamped around his ankle and yanked.

The stairs rushed up to meet him.

His head hit first.

Then darkness.

4.

The Selected

Rueben felt a sharp pain near his right eye.

He reached up, fingers grazing the crusted edge of a scab. The blood had dried, rough and cracked across his forehead. The memory hit fast—the Masked breaking into his home, the bunker exposed, the stairs rushing up to meet him.

He shot upright, eyes wide, chest heaving.

The room was unfamiliar.

He lay in a small metal bed with white sheets and a single pillow. The mattress crinkled beneath him, plastic-coated and unforgiving. He slid off slowly, trying not to make a sound, though his breath was loud in his ears.

The space was large—clinical. Seven other beds lined the wall beside him, each occupied. The bodies lay in awkward positions, limbs twisted, heads lolled. They looked like laundry dumped from a basket, not people.

At the foot of each bed sat a large trunk, identical in shape and color. Across from the beds stretched a tiled white wall, sterile and seamless, reaching all the way to the ceiling. Eight sinks were spaced evenly, one for each bed, each paired with a mirror.

Rueben stepped forward and caught his reflection.

He flinched.

His dark hair was disheveled, sticking up in uneven tufts. His green eyes were glassy, rimmed red from the gas. The gash on his forehead was smaller than it felt— just a scratch—but it throbbed with every heartbeat.

At the back of the room, a doorway broke the tiled wall.

Rueben crept toward it, breath shallow, footsteps soft. His heart pounded louder than his movements.

He rounded the corner, hoping for escape.

Instead, the room doubled back.

Behind the tiled wall, a row of white curtains hung limp. Silver showerheads jutted from the walls like cold sentinels.

This wasn't a hospital.

It wasn't a shelter.

They were in prison.

Rueben walked back into the main room, eyes scanning the sleeping bodies.

The big guy closest to him gripped the edge of the bed like it was the only thing anchoring him to reality. Veins bulged along his forearms; fingers locked in a death grip. Another figure lay curled in a tight ball, clutching the pillow like a lifeline. Rueben felt a shudder ripple through him. Something about that one seemed off—familiar, even—but the feeling unsettled him.

A girl lay diagonally across her bed, head hanging off the edge, braids spilling like ink across her face.

Then movement.

One of the figures stirred—a girl, slightly shorter than Rueben, with long dark hair cascading in soft waves over her shoulders. Her olive skin looked ghostly under the harsh fluorescent lights. Rueben couldn't help but notice how pretty she was, and the thought made his chest ache.

This wasn't the time for attraction.

Not here.

Not when only one of them would leave this place alive.

He clenched his jaw. It had to be him.

The girl sat up, eyes wide with confusion. Panic bloomed across her face. She bolted from the bed, sprinting toward a large silver door Rueben hadn't noticed before. She yanked at the handle, screamed, pounded her fists against the metal.

The room erupted.

Bodies shifted, limbs flailed, voices rose in a cacophony of fear. The Selected were waking up.

One girl scrambled onto the sinks, clawing at the ceiling tiles like escape might be hidden behind them.

Rueben stood frozen, watching the chaos unfold.

He knew better.

If the Masked could breach bunkers, they wouldn't leave this room unguarded. And they wouldn't make escape easy.

Suddenly, a shrill noise pierced the room.

The intercom crackled to life, and every movement stopped. An eerie silence fell like a blanket over the chaos. Rueben could hear the big guy trying to slow his breathing—deep, shaky inhales. A girl nearby sniffled, her sobs reduced to quiet gasps as she tried to stay silent.

Rueben looked up. The intercoms were painted to match the ceiling tiles, scattered evenly across the grid— watching, listening, hidden in plain sight.

Then the voice came.

Booming. Mechanical. Inhuman.

"Everyone line up now, introductions will take place!"

A few of them jumped. One girl whimpered. The chaos dissolved into reluctant movement.

They began to shuffle toward the beds, one by one.

The girl with the braids sat down in front of the silver door, arms crossed in defiance. Rueben caught her eye and shook his head, then pointed subtly at the cameras in the corner. He touched his forehead—just a small gesture, but it carried weight.

She rolled her eyes but stood.

The girl who had screamed earlier brushed past him, wiping tears from her cheeks. Her shoulders trembled as she took her place.

Rueben stayed quiet, listening to the voice as it continued—cold and unrelenting.

This year was different.

The 25th anniversary.

They were changing the rules.

Each player would be given an advantage: insight into their competitors. The voice droned on about transparency, strategy, and survival. Knowing why each person had been selected would reveal something about their strengths—and their weaknesses.

Rueben stared at the others.

This wasn't just a game.

It was a test.

Rueben's name echoed through the room.

He froze.

"Rueben Bentley," the voice said. "Step to the center."

His face flushed red. He felt every eye on him as he moved forward, trying not to trip over his own feet. The silence was suffocating.

The voice continued, clinical and cold.

"Rueben is known for his love of puzzle-making. He's the top escape room game master in the city—a strategist, a designer, a tactician. He's studied the Trials for years and knows each challenge like the back of his hand."

Rueben's eyes widened.

They just made me a target.

He clenched his jaw, refusing to meet the others' stares. His heart pounded in his ears. He forced his breathing to slow, forced his body to stay upright. He would not show weakness.

He walked back to his bed, each step heavier than the last.

Then another name.

Hazel Carter.

The girl with curly hair hesitated. Her eyes stayed glued to the floor, as if her shoes held the answers. Her face was bright red, and she looked like she might vomit.

Tears stained her cheeks.

She took a breath—deep, shaky—and stepped forward.

"Hazel is a computer hacker. She's worked with the FBI on high-profile cases, specializing in pattern recognition and code-breaking. She is a formidable competitor."

Rueben watched her, something twisting in his chest.

She could've been an asset. Together, they could've built the most intricate games—layered, immersive, unbeatable.

But this wasn't a partnership.

Only one of them would survive.

He felt a sharp pang of guilt. She was beautiful. Brilliant. And she would have to die for him to live.

Does she have family? Friends? A life outside this room?

Rueben shook the thought away.

He couldn't afford empathy.

Not here.

The girl with the braids was next.

"Ivy Harper," the voice announced.

She didn't move at first—just crossed her arms and narrowed her eyes at the ceiling. Rueben could already tell she wasn't going to play along quietly.

The voice continued, cynical and detached.

"Ivy is a single mother. She works full-time in a warehouse and moonlights as a server. She is resilient, resourceful, and fiercely protective.

Ivy rolled her eyes, muttering something under her breath.

Then the voice mentioned her daughter.

"Her motivation stems from her child, whom she's raised alone since birth."

Ivy snapped.

"Fuck you! Do not bring my daughter into this, you bastards!" she screamed, her voice ricocheting off the tiled walls.

Silence followed.

Not the stunned kind—more like the kind that holds its breath.

Rueben watched as the others shifted uncomfortably. One girl looked down at her feet. The big guy clenched his jaw. Ivy's rage had cracked the room open.

But the voice didn't flinch.

"Ivy learned to care for herself at an early age due to inconsistent parenting. Her survival instincts are strong, but her emotional volatility may be a liability."

Ivy began pacing, fists clenched, shoulders tight. Her braids swung with each step, like a warning.

Rueben could see it clearly—they were trying to provoke her. And it was working.

She wasn't just angry.

She was being baited.

Victor Kane was the brute from before.

Tall—around six feet—with a chiseled jawline and gorgeously tan skin that looked like it had never known weakness. Rueben felt a flicker of intimidation. Victor was built like a statue, all muscle and menace.

His hair was cropped short, military-style, and his bright blue eyes gleamed with intensity. His arms were thick with tribal tattoos, inked in bold patterns that made him look even more formidable.

The voice overhead began its announcement.

"Victor Kane is a former Marine. He now works as a personal trainer. His physical strength and combat experience make him a formidable contender."

Victor's smile grew with every word.

Rueben watched, uneasy. They were feeding this man's ego like it was part of the game.

He thought about Marine training—how brutal it must've been. The psychological warfare. The conditioning. Had Victor seen combat? Had he killed without hesitation?

Rueben's mind spun with possibilities.

Victor could be useful. If they teamed up, his battle instincts could be an asset. His ruthlessness might be the edge they needed.

For a moment, Rueben allowed himself to imagine it—survival through alliance. Maybe they didn't all have to die. Maybe there was a way out.

Then Victor spoke.

And shattered the illusion.

"All of you puny bitches are going to lose, and I'll be going home to my family," Victor said, his voice steady and smug.

Not a hint of doubt.

Rueben couldn't help but smirk. The guy was practically dripping arrogance. He could feel Victor's eyes on him, ready to fire back—but before he could speak, Ivy stepped in.

"I'll fight for my daughter," she snapped. "And if that means taking out the competition, then I'd watch my back if I were you. You can't take all of us."

Her voice cracked slightly, but she didn't flinch.

Rueben turned to her, stunned.

She had no fear.

And somehow, that made him feel responsible. Protective.

He clenched his fists, jaw tight.

Why am I trying to help strangers? he thought. This isn't a team. It's survival.

He looked around the room—Hazel still wiping her eyes, Victor puffed up like a peacock, Ivy pacing like a caged animal.

He needed to focus.

Hopefully, the Trials didn't start immediately. He needed rest. Time to think. The stress was pressing down on him like a weight, and his body was starting to feel it—tight muscles, foggy thoughts, a headache blooming behind his eyes.

Rueben sat down slowly, trying to center himself.

He couldn't afford distraction.

Not now.

The rest of the group passed by in a haze.

Rueben barely registered the names.

Natalie—a bank manager. Compared to the others, her profile felt... underwhelming. No combat training, no hacking skills. Just spreadsheets and vaults.

Then Hank—a handyperson at a local hotel chain. Quiet, broad-shouldered, with grease-stained fingers and a nervous twitch in his jaw.

Trinity was next. A police officer. She looked the part—rigid posture, sharp eyes. Rueben guessed she'd been on her way to work when they took her. Her holster was empty, but the imprint of her badge still clung to her belt.

Then the final name.

Rueben didn't catch it.

He was pulled from his trance by a wave of unease that rippled through the room.

Everyone had gone still.

Victor's smirk faded. His jaw tightened.

Rueben turned to look—and felt his stomach drop.

The man stood alone, silent, unmoving. There was something wrong with him. Not visibly. Not physically. But the air around him felt heavier, like it had been poisoned.

Even Ivy shifted closer to Rueben, her defiance momentarily quieted.

No one spoke.

No one moved.

They were all thinking the same thing.

Why would they leave us alone in a room with him?

The last player stepped forward. Rueben knew who he was immediately.

Silas Thorn.

A small, thin man with a crooked spine and a face like dried leather—tight, cracked, and hardened by time. His eyes were sunken, but sharp. Watching. Waiting.

Rueben's breath caught.

His chest tightened.

He knew that face, he could never forget it.

His blood turned to ice.

Silas smiled wide, lips stretched unnaturally, and let out a low, spine-chilling chuckle that echoed through the sterile room.

The voice overhead spoke without emotion.

"Silas Thorn is a convicted serial killer. Known for gutting his victims and consuming their hearts. He evaded capture for years. Highly dangerous. Highly unstable."

The silence that followed was suffocating.

No one moved.

Victor's bravado cracked. Ivy's fists trembled. Hazel took a step back.

But Rueben didn't move.

He couldn't.

His legs felt like stone. His vision blurred. The tiled walls seemed to close in.

Memories stirred—ones he'd buried deep. News reports. Headlines. A courtroom sketch. A voice he'd tried to forget.

He had spent years trying to erase Silas Thorn from his mind.

And now he was here.

Smiling.

Rueben clenched his fists so tightly his nails dug into his palms.

This wasn't just survival anymore.

This was personal.

5.

The Killer

A whirlwind of panic tore through the room.

Ivy's defiant bravado shattered in an instant. She stumbled backward, nearly tripping over her own feet, her eyes locked on Silas. She had been standing closest when the announcement dropped—when the name Silas Thorn turned the air to ice.

Trinity reached instinctively for her hip, fingers grasping at an empty holster. Her face was pale, her training overridden by raw fear.

Victor snapped out of his stupor with a roar. He lunged forward, grabbing Silas by the throat and slamming him into the tiled floor. Their heads landed dangerously close to the row of sinks, the metal echoing with the impact.

Silas didn't fight back.

He just smiled.

Then the intercom crackled to life again, slicing through the chaos.

"PLEASE DO NOT KILL THE OTHER PLAYERS UNTIL THE TRIALS BEGIN. EVERY SINGLE ONE OF YOU IS CRUCIAL TO THE GAMES. YOU MUST PLAY BY THE RULES IN ORDER TO SAVE HUMANITY FROM CERTAIN PERIL."

The room froze.

Victor hesitated, his grip still tight around Silas's neck. Rueben could see the conflict in his eyes—rage battling obedience.

Then, as if summoned by the voice itself, the Masked entered.

Brutish figures filled the corners of the room, emerging from hidden panels and shadowed alcoves. Their demon masks gleamed under the fluorescent lights—horned, angular, grotesque. Each one held a baton or a rifle, silent and still, like statues waiting to strike.

Rueben's breath caught.

They weren't just guards.

They were predators.

Watching.

Waiting.

Rueben stood frozen.

The Masked had placed them in a room with a psychotic murderer—and expected them to play by the rules.

He scanned the others. Ivy had retreated to the far wall, her bravado cracked and leaking. Trinity still clutched at her empty holster, eyes wide and unblinking. Victor, seething, slammed his fist into the tiled wall with a roar.

The impact echoed.

Shards of ceramic scattered across the floor.

Victor pulled his hand back, revealing a trail of blood trickling down his knuckles. A crimson streak smeared across the white wall—bright, violent, wrong.

Rueben's breath hitched.

The blood unearthed something buried deep inside him. A memory. A night he had locked away.

He had been out late, partying with friends. Fresh out of high school, riding the high of freedom. His freshman year had just begun, and he'd chosen a local university to stay close to home, save money, keep things simple.

It was spring break.

The city was on edge—killings, curfews, warnings on every news channel. But Rueben had brushed it off. He told his mother he'd be fine. That he'd be surrounded by people. That he'd have friends stay over so he wouldn't walk home alone.

She had hesitated.

He had smiled.

And then he left.

Now, standing in this sterile room with blood on the walls and monsters in masks, Rueben felt the weight of that night pressing down on him like a vice.

He clenched his fists.

If I had stayed home...

Maybe then—

Rueben stared at the blood streaking down the wall, his breath shallow.

Something inside him shifted.

Not just fear—something older. Something buried.

The room around him blurred, the fluorescent lights flickering like distant stars. He felt the weight of a memory pressing against his chest, demanding to be seen.

He didn't want to go back.

But he was already there.

"The police have no new leads, as they continue their search for the brutal serial slayer terrorizing the city…"

The news anchor's voice droned from the bar's overhead screen, barely registering in Rueben's mind as he waited for his drink. The clink of glasses, the hum of conversation, the pulse of music—all of it blurred into background noise.

"The Crimson Gorger is still at large, and investigators are asking for any information that can help with the investigation. If you have anything that can help, please contact law enforcement at 983-42—"

The voice cut off.

The memory began to fade.

Rueben tried to push it down, tried to stay anchored in the now.

But Silas was staring at him.

That grin—wide, unnatural, carved into his face like a mask—hadn't moved. His eyes locked onto Rueben's with a quiet hunger.

Rueben's stomach dropped.

His throat tightened.

He choked back a cry as the memories surged forward, uninvited, and merciless. The bar. The broadcast. The flicker of fear he hadn't understood at the time.

He had heard the name before.

He had seen the face.

And now, the past was staring back at him.

Alive.

It was nearly two in the morning when they finally decided to head home.

Rueben and his closest friend, Tyler, walked side by side down the empty street, their laughter from earlier now faded into quiet conversation. The night had grown colder, and Rueben tugged his jacket tighter around his shoulders.

He glanced up at the streetlight—the one his mother had written about in her letters to the city. She'd begged them to fix it, to stop it from flickering, from plunging the block into darkness every few minutes.

It was off now.

The entire stretch of road was swallowed in shadow, forcing the boys to use their phone flashlights to navigate the cracked pavement ahead. The beams bounced off broken glass and uneven concrete, casting long, distorted shadows that danced with every step.

Rueben felt a chill crawl up his spine.

Something about the silence didn't feel right.

They had almost reached Rueben's house when the sound hit them.

A rush of footsteps—fast, erratic, barreling toward them from the shadows.

Rueben instinctively flipped his phone upward, the flashlight beam slicing through the dark. A figure emerged—thin, wild-eyed, moving with unnatural speed. His clothes were soaked in something slick and dark, glistening under the light like oil. But it wasn't oil.

Rueben couldn't breathe.

The man slammed into his shoulder, hard enough to knock him sideways. Rueben spun, ready to confront him—but froze.

Blood.

It was smeared across the man's shirt, thick and fresh. His wide eyes locked onto Rueben's, and for a moment, time fractured.

Then the man threw his head back and laughed.

Not a chuckle.

A cackle.

Unhinged. Joyful. Inhuman.

Rueben's stomach dropped.

He didn't know who the man was.

But he knew what he was.

Danger.

Tyler had shouted, "I'm going to call the police."

And just like that, the man turned and bolted down the street, vanishing into the dark like smoke.

Rueben had felt a flicker of relief then—brief, fragile. Tyler still clutched his phone like a weapon as they turned toward home, their steps quick and quiet. The rest of the walk blurred into silence, both boys trying to make sense of what had just happened. Rueben remembered the way his heart had pounded, the way his skin had felt too tight, like it didn't belong to him.

Now, back in the present, Rueben blinked hard.

Snap out of it, he told himself.

You're in the Trials.

Any sign of weakness, and the others would turn on him in a heartbeat. He'd seen it before—in games, in life. Fear had a way of peeling people back to their worst selves.

He clenched his jaw and forced his breathing to steady.

There was no room for panic.

Not anymore.

Silas was still staring.

Unblinking. Unmoving.

Rueben felt his stomach twist, his throat tightening like a noose. He swallowed hard, but the nausea lingered. His palms were slick with sweat, and he could feel the tremor in his fingers. He took a step back, slow, and deliberate, hoping no one noticed the fear clawing across his face.

Does he know who I am?

He couldn't.

Does he recognize me from that night?

Silas's grin widened, stretching unnaturally across his face. He lifted a finger and dragged it across the blood smeared on the wall—Victor's blood. The red streak glistened on his fingertip.

Then, without breaking eye contact, he pressed it to his lips.

Smearing it like ChapStick.

Rueben's breath caught.

Silas raked his tongue across his mouth, slow and deliberate, closing his eyes as if savoring the taste. A low hum escaped his throat—pleasure, mockery, madness.

Victor's fists clenched at his sides. His whole body was taut, vibrating with rage. Rueben could see the war behind his eyes—morality versus instinct, restraint versus violence.

He wanted to strike.

Everyone could feel it.

But Rueben couldn't look away.

The scene twisted in his mind, warping into something older, something buried. The blood. The grin. The eyes.

He was being pulled under.

Back into the nightmare.

They were just steps from Rueben's house when he saw it.

The front door.

Standing wide open.

His stomach lurched, rising into his throat like a warning. He stopped cold, eyes scanning the porch, the windows, the yard—searching for movement, for a shadow, for any sign of his mother.

Maybe she'd heard the man laughing in the street.

Maybe she'd come out to check.

Maybe—

But the porch light was off.

No silhouette in the doorway.

No voice calling his name.

Just silence.

Rueben took a shaky breath, trying to steady himself. Tyler said something, but it didn't register. The world had narrowed to that open door and the hollow space behind it.

His mother was nowhere to be seen.

And something was wrong.

Rueben sprinted to the front door, heart hammering, voice cracking as he screamed his mother's name.

No response.

The porch light glowed softly behind him, casting long shadows across the steps. But inside, the house was dark—eerily so. Only one light flickered from upstairs, pale and distant.

He stepped inside, flicking on the foyer lights with trembling fingers. The familiar glow spilled across the hardwood floor, illuminating the shoes he always left in front of the stairs. He dodged them out of habit, but everything felt wrong—too quiet, too still.

He bounded up the stairs, two at a time, breath shallow, panic rising like floodwater.

Still no sound.

No movement.

No voice.

His mother wasn't answering.

And something was very, very wrong.

He reached the top of the stairs and turned toward the light spilling from the right side of the hall.

It was coming from her room.

The door was cracked open, just enough to reveal the edge of the bedside table—and that lamp.

The old vintage one with the shade of green glass.

It cast a sickly glow across the hallway, tinting the wallpaper and floorboards in hues that felt wrong. Rueben had always hated that lamp. The way it distorted everything. The way it made shadows look deeper than they were.

But his mother loved it.

She said it had belonged to her grandfather. That it was sturdy. Reliable. That it had survived decades of storms and moves and grief.

Rueben swallowed hard.

The lamp was still on.

But the room was silent.

Rueben ran to the door and looked in.

The sight knocked the breath from his lungs.

He dropped to his knees, a scream tearing from his throat—anguish, disbelief, horror all tangled into one sound that didn't feel human.

His mother lay sprawled across the bed, her body limp, surrounded by a pool of blood that soaked into the sheets and dripped onto the floor. The walls behind her were splattered—violent, chaotic, like something had exploded from within.

The green glow from the vintage lamp cast everything in sickly shadows. The blood looked almost black under its light, thick and glistening as it seeped from the gaping wound in her chest.

Her heart was gone.

Taken.

She was the eighth victim of *The Crimson Gorger*.

Rueben couldn't move.

Couldn't breathe.

The room felt like it was closing in, pressing against his ribs, crushing him from the inside out.

The sound of metal gears scraping snapped Rueben back to reality.

He wiped a tear from his cheek, his fingers trembling as he forced himself to focus. The grief still clung to him like smoke, but the room had changed.

In the center, the floor had split open with mechanical precision. A long white table rose slowly from the void, its surface gleaming under the harsh lights. Eight colored vials sat in a perfect row—each one glowing faintly, like they held something alive.

Movement caught his eye.

The Masked were in motion now, gliding across the room with eerie synchronicity. One by one, they handed each player a white envelope, names scrawled in jagged ink across the front.

Rueben took his without a word.

His name stared back at him.

The Trials were beginning.

And there was no turning back.

6.

Vials

Rueben stared at the eight vials, their colors pulsing faintly like they were breathing.

He looked down at the envelope in his hand, fingers twitching against the paper. His heart was pounding—too fast, too loud. He didn't understand why. The first trial was statistically always the easiest. He'd watched dozens of recordings, dissected strategies, even ran mock simulations in his head. If he'd been in the games before now, he was certain he could've passed every single one.

But watching and surviving were two different things.

Now, the stakes were real.

His life was on the line.

And the irony wasn't lost on him—how humiliating would it be if he, the escape room game master, was the first to die in the Trials?

Victor moved first.

He tore open his envelope with a sneer, scanned the contents, then scoffed loudly. Without hesitation, he marched across the room, stopping directly in front of the camera and the Masked who had retreated to guard the door.

He locked eyes with the largest one.

Then, slowly, deliberately, he shredded the letter into tiny pieces, letting them rain into his palm like confetti.

Rueben's breath caught.

Victor leaned forward—and blew the shards directly into the Masked's face.

It was bold.

It was stupid.

It was Victor.

The movement was so fast Rueben almost didn't register it.

One second, Victor was blowing shredded paper into the Masked's face.

The next, he was on the ground.

With a single, fluid motion, the brute had swept Victor's legs out from under him and slammed him down, pinning him with a thick black boot pressed against his throat. The impact echoed through the room, sharp and final.

Trinity let out a startled squeal, her hand flying to her mouth.

Ivy didn't flinch. She was trying hard to hide a smirk, but Rueben caught it—just a flicker of satisfaction in her eyes.

Victor's face was twisted in shock. Not pain. Not fear.

Just disbelief.

Rueben felt something unexpected stir in his chest.

Amusement.

It was fleeting, but real.

Victor had taunted the people who kidnapped them—and now he was learning exactly how little power he had here.

The intercom crackled again, louder this time.

"THERE WILL BE NO INTIMIDATION TACTICS FROM ANY OF YOU. STAY IN YOUR PLACE OR YOU WILL BE REPLACED. YOUR LIVES ARE MEANINGLESS TO US. NOW, READ

YOUR WELCOME LETTER AND LET THE TRIALS COMMENCE."

The boot lifted.

Victor coughed, rolling onto his side.

No one moved.

Rueben looked down at his envelope again.

It was time.

The intercom crackled again, sharper this time—like static laced with contempt.

"YOU WERE CHOSEN FOR YOUR FLAWS, NOT YOUR STRENGTHS. YOUR ARROGANCE. YOUR DESPERATION. YOUR SECRETS. WE KNOW THEM ALL."

"ONE OF YOU WILL DIE. THAT IS NOT A THREAT. IT IS A REQUIREMENT."

The intercom clicked off.

Rueben felt the air shift.

The Trials had truly begun.

Rueben could tell the announcer was getting annoyed with the group and he could not help but wonder what others in the past had done. Had any tried to fight back, or were they all just too brazen for their own good?

Rueben opened the letter and tried to control his facial reactions as he read.

Welcome to the Trials Rueben,

You have been hand selected for the trials for your expertise in creating games like the ones you are about to play. Sitting in front of you are eight vials. They are assorted like the rainbow to make them appear less harmful than they are. One vial contains a fast-acting poison, while the others are safe to drink. You can change the outcome of this game by selecting the right person to eliminate. One must die for you all to proceed. Solve this riddle to survive.

The poison attacks your spleen.

Causing immense pain

Red, yellow, blue, green

Let us make blood rain.

Solve the riddle and live or take a chance with a guess. The choice is yours.

Good Luck,

H.C. Game Master Assistant

Rueben was hand-selected for his gaming expertise.

The words echoed in his mind like a warning.

What did that mean for the games this time around? Were they going to be harder—tailored to his strengths just to break him? Had the Masked been watching him, tracking his habits, logging the hours he spent dissecting trial footage in the dark corners of the internet?

Were the others also chosen?

Had they received cryptic messages too—signed by some faceless authority Rueben now assumed was a high council?

He scanned the room.

Hazel was still reading, her eyes flicking back and forth like she was stuck in a loop, trying to decode something that refused to make sense.

Ivy sat curled up in the corner, shoulders trembling, tears slipping down her cheeks. She was trying to hide it, but Rueben saw the grief etched into her face. Had they threatened her daughter? Or was the letter simply making everything real?

And then there was Silas.

Still smiling.

Like this was a game.

Like he couldn't wait for the chaos to begin.

Rueben glanced down at his feet.

A small scrap of paper was tucked beneath his shoe—one of the pieces Victor had shredded in his act of defiance. He bent down and picked it up, flipping it over, eyes scanning for anything useful.

It was typed.

Clean, uniform, impersonal.

Rueben's stomach sank.

His own letter had been handwritten—inked in jagged strokes that felt deliberate, intimate. Someone had taken the time to write it. To choose their words. To speak directly to him.

Victor's letter was mass-produced.

Generic.

That meant something.

Someone had singled Rueben out.

Not just for his gaming expertise—but for something more.

Help?

Manipulation?

He didn't know.

But it changed everything.

Rueben folded the scrap and slipped it into his pocket.

He needed to stay sharp.

Because someone was watching.

And they weren't following the rules.

Rueben looked back at the table in the center of the room.

The vials were arranged like a rainbow—bright, clean, almost cheerful. They looked more like flavored drinks than something deadly. That was the point, wasn't it? To make them seem harmless. To lull them into a false sense of choice.

The riddle looped in his head like static.

"Let's make blood rain."

His eyes drifted to the red vial. It looked like Kool-Aid. Maybe the poison caused internal bleeding—blood pouring from the mouth like in horror films. That would fit the imagery. Blood rain.

But something didn't sit right.

He scanned the colors again: red, yellow, blue, green.

Four colors.

Was the answer the fourth one—green?

That felt too simple. Too literal.

He looked again at the words in the riddle.

Pain. Rain.

Both rhymed. Both had four letters.

Only one color in the list matched that pattern.

Blue.

Rueben's breath caught.

It wasn't about order.

It was about structure.

The blue vial.

That was the poison.

Rueben felt a flicker of relief.

He could survive this round.

He was sure of it now—the riddle, the logic, the blue vial. It all lined up. But the relief was short-lived. As he looked around at the others—Hazel was still rereading her letter, Ivy quietly crying, Silas grinning like a child at a carnival—guilt twisted in his chest.

He was the only one who knew.

The poison's location.

The fate of the group rested in his hands alone.

How was he supposed to carry that?

Maybe he could make the first move. Drink one of the vials. Let the rest of them figure it out from there. It would be bold. It would be dangerous. But it would shift the pressure.

Rueben stepped toward the table.

Each vial gleamed under the lights, innocent and deadly.

He reached out.

And hesitated.

"I hope you know that we have to make a decision together," Ivy said, her voice sharp, her eyes narrowing with disdain.

Rueben avoided her gaze. "I just figured we'd all pick a vial and drink it," he muttered, trying not to look at the blue one.

Hazel spoke softly from the corner. "I feel like if we all try and work together, maybe more of us can survive than in the past."

Rueben looked at her, sadness flickering in his eyes.

She didn't know.

None of them did.

He'd studied these games. He knew the pattern. One trial, one death. The math was cruel and simple. Only one of them would leave alive.

He sighed.

If he wanted to survive, he had to play along—for now. Later, when fewer people stood in his way, he could shift tactics.

"Fine," he said. "We can try to work together. But how do we know which vial is the poison?"

"The red one makes the most sense," Victor said confidently. "It's the color of blood."

"That's too obvious," Trinity countered. "They aren't that dumb. Maybe the purple one. You can't see what's swirling inside."

"What if it's the yellow one?" Natalie offered from the back. Rueben had almost forgotten she was there. "It's the most unassuming."

"I think it might be the green one," Hank said. "It's usually the color of health drinks. It'd be ironic if that's the one that kills. The color of life."

Rueben turned to Hank, startled. The handyman's insight was unexpected—wrong, maybe, but thoughtful. This wasn't going to be easy. These weren't just victims. They were thinkers. Survivors.

And yet, only one would make it.

Rueben's eyes drifted to Silas.

The man who had taken his mother's life.

If anyone deserved to die, it was him.

Rueben clenched his jaw and shook his head.

No.

He couldn't think like that.

It was wrong.

He was better than this.

He had to be.

"Which vial were you about to drink, Mr. Game Master?" Silas asked, his voice slick with amusement.

He was staring directly at Rueben, that never-ending smirk plastered across his face like a mask he refused to take off.

Rueben's stomach churned.

That smile made him uneasy. It made him angry. Why was this jerk always so smug? So sure of himself?

Everyone was watching now.

Rueben scanned the room—Hazel, Ivy, Trinity, Victor, Hank, Natalie. All eyes on him. He had seconds to decide.

"What?" he asked, stalling.

If he said the wrong vial, would Silas call his bluff? Force him to drink it? Or worse—drink it himself and die, giving Rueben the revenge he'd secretly craved?

Could Rueben live with that?

He thought of his mother. Of her empty chair at his college graduation. Of the blood. Of the lamp.

His jaw clenched.

He didn't care anymore.

This was his moment.

Silas repeated the question.

Rueben met his gaze.

"Blue," he said, steadying his voice. "I was going to drink the blue one before they all stopped me."

That was all Silas needed to hear.

He must have trusted Rueben's judgment—as an escape room master, as someone who understood games. He took two long strides to the table, grabbed the blue vial, twisted the cap, and downed it in one gulp.

For a moment, nothing happened.

Everyone held their breath.

Silas grinned wider, lips parting to speak—

Then the gurgling started.

His eyes widened. The smile vanished.

White foam crested his lips as he gasped for air, clawing at his throat, shoving his fingers into his mouth, desperate to purge the poison. He coughed, and blood erupted through the foam, staining his chin, his shirt, the floor.

His blue eyes locked onto Rueben's.

There was betrayal in them.

And guilt.

Rueben felt it hit him like a punch to the gut.

Silas crumpled, convulsing, blood splattering in jagged arcs. With a final choke and a soft gurgle, he stilled.

Rueben couldn't move.

The blood crept toward him like a hand reaching out in the dark.

He felt frozen—awake and asleep at the same time. A nightmare with no exit.

Fear and guilt swirled inside him.

Silas was dead.

And Rueben had killed him.

7.

Cleanup

Rueben was overcome with dread.

And guilt.

How could he have killed someone?

He put his head in his hands, gripping his hair so tightly his scalp burned. He wanted to tear it out, to punish himself, to feel something other than the hollow ache in his chest.

But he didn't.

He had to trust the process.

Silas was a murderer. He deserved it. Who knew what he would've done to the rest of them in their sleep?

Hazel stood beside him; her eyes locked on the body. She kept glancing between Silas and Rueben, her jaw clenched, fists balled so tight her knuckles had gone white.

She knew.

She had to.

She worked with the FBI, didn't she? She'd seen killers before. She could read people. It was only a matter of time before she outed his secret.

Would the group hate him?

Or would they thank him?

"The Crimson Gorger is dead," he thought. *"But I'm the one who killed him."*

"That would've been you," Ivy said quietly, sitting down on one of the beds.

She hadn't taken her eyes off Silas.

Victor seemed unshaken.

He knelt beside Silas's body, eyes scanning the frothy mess still leaking from the man's mouth. Blood pooled beneath him, but Victor didn't flinch. Maybe his military training was kicking in—analyzing the poison, cataloging symptoms. Or maybe he was just... off.

Too calm.

Too curious.

Rueben watched him closely.

Victor's fingers hovered near Silas's jaw, not touching, just observing. Like he was studying a specimen. Like he'd seen this before.

Rueben swallowed hard.

"I'm a little grateful he drank that in my place," he said aloud, voice low. "He had too much confidence in me."

It was a deflection.

A weak one.

Was his voice shaking?

Probably.

But then again, a man had just died in front of them. Maybe no one would notice the guilt buried beneath his words.

Maybe.

He felt it before he saw it.

That prickling sensation—like eyes crawling across his skin.

Rueben glanced up and locked eyes with Hazel.

She was staring at him now. Not casually. Not curiously.

Intently.

She looked once more at Silas's body, then back at Rueben, her brow furrowed, lips pressed into a thin line. The wheels were turning, and Rueben could feel them grinding toward him.

Then he saw Trinity.

The police officer.

She was watching him too.

Great. Just what he needed—two of the sharpest minds in the room dissecting him like a crime scene.

Rueben looked down at his shoes, tugging at the hem of his shirt like a nervous tic.

If they knew his secret… maybe they also knew the truth.

Silas was dangerous.

And now, he was gone.

Rueben thought of his mother.

Of the lamp.

Of the blood.

And for just a moment, satisfaction bloomed in his chest.

Justice.

Finally.

Rueben did not like thinking of his mother often. The memory of her death was almost too bearable for him. He hated that he lived in the house where it had happened, but he also could not force himself to move. There were too many good memories in that house, memories that outweighed the horrific events that had taken place. Shortly after his mother had been found, his father decided he was going to move to the other side of the country and shack up with some young blonde to ease the pain. He said he just needed *"a fresh start."* The last good thing his father did before leaving was give him the house. Rueben could not blame him for getting away, but he also loved to see the rose bush his mother planted in the front yard bloom every spring.

He closed his eyes, just for a second, and imagined the rose bush in bloom. The way the petals curled like paper, the way the scent lingered in the morning air.

But the copper stung his nose.

The blood was real.

And he couldn't afford to drift.

Not here.

Not now.

The screeching of metal drew the group's attention to the door.

Three of the Masked entered, broad-shouldered and towering, each one clad in black track suits with white stripes down the sides. Their boots squelched in Silas's blood, leaving crimson prints across the tile. The devil masks they wore gleamed under the fluorescent lights— bright white teeth grinning through the gore.

Two of them grabbed Silas by the shoulders. The third took his legs.

They lifted him without a word.

Rueben felt a chill crawl down his spine. The calmness of it—the efficiency—was worse than the violence.

Then Ivy moved.

She darted toward the open door, a blur of desperation.

Just as she reached the threshold, another Masked stepped into view.

She slammed into him and bounced off like a rag doll, hitting the floor hard.

As she scrambled to rise, her hands slipped in the blood.

She looked down.

Dark red stained her arms, her palms, her clothes.

Her breath caught.

She was part of it now.

Marked.

"Now why did you think they'd leave the doorway unguarded?" Victor asked, trying—and failing—to wipe the smirk off his face.

"A girl can dream, can't she?" Ivy replied, her voice trembling, but her spirit still flickering beneath the fear.

From the back, Hank chuckled.

Rueben couldn't help it—he cracked a smile.

Then, like a dam breaking, they all burst out laughing.

It wasn't joy.

It was survival.

Rueben hadn't realized how tense he'd been until the laughter hit him like a wave. His shoulders loosened. His jaw unclenched. For a moment, the blood on the floor didn't matter. The Trials didn't matter.

They were just people.

Trying to stay human.

BOOM.

A loud bang echoed through the mostly empty room, reverberating off the tile and slicing through the air like a scythe.

The door had been flung open so hard it slammed against the wall with a metallic crack.

Rueben and the others froze mid-laugh, heads snapping toward the sound.

A figure stood in the doorway.

Clad in a stark yellow hazmat suit, black knee-high boots gleaming under the fluorescent lights. A gas mask obscured their face, the round lenses catching the overhead glare like insect eyes.

Then another figure entered, wheeling a rusty cart. The wheels squealed with every rotation, the sound sharp and grating.

With a gloved hand, the first figure pointed to the cart.

Then to the blood-soaked floor.

The top tier held bottles of bleach.

The bottom was stuffed with cloths—gray, shapeless, institutional.

Three mop heads hung from the side, still wrapped in cellophane.

White.

Untouched.

For now.

It was an unspoken agreement now—their captors were stronger. Faster. Bigger. Even Victor looked small next to them, and that was saying something.

Rueben couldn't help but wonder how they'd found a group of men all built the same. Broad shoulders.

Towering frames. Identical masks. Like they'd been manufactured, not born.

The group began the cleanup in silence.

The crinkle of cellophane echoed through the room, unnaturally loud against the stillness.

Hazel was the first to speak.

"They didn't give us any mop buckets," she murmured, more to herself than anyone else.

Rueben scanned the room. Eight sinks. Seven survivors.

He grabbed a rag and a bottle of bleach from the cart and walked to the farthest sink—the one closest to where Silas had died.

He stuffed the rag into the rusted drain and turned the tap.

A groan echoed behind the wall.

Water sputtered out, tinged brown, then cleared.

Steam rose.

Rueben poured in the bleach.

It nearly overflowed.

But it would work.

The rest of the group began to move slowly, mechanically.

Ivy sloshed her rag across the floor, barely trying. The blood soaked into her sleeves, her skin, but she didn't flinch anymore. She was past that. Past caring. Past resisting.

Rueben tried to mop, but the blood just smeared—thick, stubborn, refusing to be erased. It clung to the tile like memory. Like guilt.

Frustration bubbled in his chest.

The smell of bleach was overwhelming. Sharp. Familiar.

And then the sound—dripping water.

He was back in that room.

The bathroom. His parents' house. The silence after the sirens. The way the light had hit the broken lamp. The way the blood had pooled beneath her head. The way he'd scrubbed at the floor, not because anyone asked him to, but because he couldn't stop.

He'd cleaned for hours.

Not to erase the evidence.

But to erase the moment.

No.

He blinked hard.

He wasn't at home.

This was worse.

This was engineered.

And Rueben was the one holding the mop.

He looked down at his hands. They were trembling. Not from fear. From memory. From the weight of it all.

He thought of the rose bush.

Of spring.

Of the way it bloomed despite everything.

He thought of his father, packing bags, chasing a fresh start with a woman half his age.

He thought of the house. The silence. The ache.

Rueben pressed the mop harder into the floor, as if force could make the blood disappear.

It didn't.

It just spread.

He was cleaning a crime scene again.

Only this time, he wasn't the witness.

He was the reason.

Rueben looked around the room, hoping no one had noticed how deeply he'd slipped into his own thoughts.

Hazel was still working near the spot where Silas had fallen, her movements methodical, almost reverent. Trinity was scrubbing her hands raw, trying to erase the blood that had stained her skin—and maybe something deeper. Ivy muttered to herself as she cleaned near the doorway, her voice low and fractured. Hank was at the sink again, pouring more bleach, his face unreadable.

Then Rueben saw Victor.

Just sitting.

Perched on the edge of his bed like nothing had happened.

"Thanks for all the help," Rueben said, his voice laced with disdain.

Victor smirked. "I'm tired. It's been a stressful day."

Rueben shook his head and turned away.

He didn't have the energy to argue.

He just wanted to sleep.

The rest of the group finished the cleanup in silence, each one casting a glance at Victor—who was now snoring softly, untouched by the blood, untouched by the guilt.

Once the last bit of blood had been scrubbed from the tile, Rueben couldn't help but wonder if the room was cleaner than when they'd first arrived. It gleamed now—bleached, sterile, hollow. Like a crime scene that had been erased but not forgotten.

The Masked men in yellow rubber suits returned, silent as ever. They collected the supplies with mechanical precision, then came back moments later with a stack of folded clothes. One set for each bed.

No words. No instructions.

Just expectation.

Grumbling under their breath, the group took turns showering behind the wall. The water was lukewarm, the soap industrial, the towels thin and scratchy. But it was something. A ritual. A reset.

They all emerged wearing the same thing—black sweatpants, grey T-shirts, slip-on shoes. Uniform. Identical. Stripped of identity, stripped of blood.

Rueben stared at the others.

They looked like inmates.

Or patients.

Or ghosts.

He picked the bed in the far corner, the one furthest from the door, and laid down. The mattress was thin, the blanket stiff, but he didn't care. His body ached. His mind buzzed.

The room was quiet now.

Too quiet.

He listened to the dripping of the sink. Slow. Rhythmic. Like a metronome counting down to something he couldn't see.

He closed his eyes.

But sleep didn't come gently.

It dragged him under.

And in that darkness, Rueben saw the rose bush blooming in spring.

Then the lamp.

Then the blood.

Then Silas's eyes.

Wide.

Accusing.

Rueben flinched in his sleep.

The Trials weren't over.

They were just beginning.

8.

The Reunion

Rueben felt an overwhelming sense of loneliness and despair as he sat on the floor, his head buried in his hands.

The room was white.

Not painted white—consumed by it.

There were no walls. No corners. No shadows. Just endless, blinding light that pressed against his skin like static. He couldn't tell if he was sitting or floating. The ground beneath him felt soft, but not solid. Like memory. Like fog.

His lungs burned.

There was no air here. No sound. No warmth.

It felt like space—silent, infinite, indifferent.

He tried to breathe, but each inhale felt thinner than the last. Panic clawed at his chest, but even that felt muted, like it was happening to someone else.

The stark white made his eyes water. He blinked rapidly, searching for something—anything—to anchor himself. A shape. A shadow. A voice.

Nothing.

Just light.

He reached out, fingers trembling, hoping to touch something real. But his hand disappeared into the brightness, swallowed whole.

He was alone.

Utterly.

And then he heard it.

A faint dripping.

Steady. Rhythmic. Familiar.

The sink.

The one from the room.

The one from home.

Rueben turned his head, but the sound came from everywhere and nowhere. It echoed inside him, like a memory trying to claw its way back.

He whispered into the void, voice cracking.

"Mom?"

No answer.

Just the drip.

And the white.

Rueben was completely alone.

Or so he thought.

The whispers came first—soft, slithering, curling around him like smoke. They came from everywhere and nowhere, impossible to trace.

"You did this," one hissed, dripping with venom.

Rueben winced.

"It's all YOUR fault," another spat, louder, crueler.

His eyes darted around the blinding white space, searching for the source. But the room had no edges, no walls—just light. Endless, suffocating light.

Then the shadows formed.

Dark tendrils stretched from the corners, reaching for him. But there were no corners. The shadows were inventing them, carving space out of nothing. They slithered across the floor, slow and deliberate, like they knew he couldn't run.

Rueben tried to move, inching forward, but the light pulsed violently, and the voices multiplied.

Some were sobbing.

Others were screaming.

A chorus of grief and rage, crashing over him like a tidal wave.

"You killed him."

"You let it happen."

"She's gone because of you."

The words blurred together, overlapping, impossible to separate. Rueben clutched his head, trying to block them out, but they were inside him now—echoing through his bones.

Flashes of light exploded in his vision, white-hot and searing. Each burst brought a new scream, a new accusation. The guttural sounds twisted into something inhuman—like the room itself was howling.

Rueben fell to his knees.

The shadows closed in.

And the light kept flashing.

And the voices kept screaming.

And Rueben couldn't tell if he was dreaming anymore.

Or remembering.

Rueben rubbed his eyes, but the light only grew harsher.

The room was shifting—walls bending, corners stretching, the floor rippling like water beneath him. A loud shriek tore through the space, sharp and primal, forcing him to clamp his hands over his ears. He squeezed his eyes shut, bracing for impact, for pain, for whatever presence he now felt pressing in around him.

Footsteps echoed—slow, deliberate, cascading across tile that hadn't been there before.

He opened his eyes, squinting against the brightness. Only the corners offered relief, patches of shadow that pulsed like breathing lungs.

"Who's there?" he croaked, trying to sound confident, but his voice betrayed him—thin, cracked, afraid.

The voices surged louder, overlapping, crashing into each other like waves. Still, the footsteps persisted. Closer. Closer.

Then a flash.

Blinding.

And suddenly, shapes filled the room. A couch. A lamp. A picture frame. Familiar outlines blurred by light.

Rueben blinked hard.

"IT'S YOUR FAULT," a voice growled in his ear—deep, guttural, too close.

He jumped, heart hammering, the hair on his arms standing straight.

The light began to fade, dissolving like mist in a movie scene. The whiteness peeled away, revealing color, texture, and memory.

He looked around.

He was home.

***

He glanced around the all-too-familiar room.

He was standing in the middle of his childhood home.

Everything was exactly as he remembered it—down to the placement of the furniture, the cracks in the windows, the way the sunlight filtered in like a memory trying to be reborn. But something was off. The sheer shine of everything made it feel... polished. Preserved. Like a museum exhibit of his past.

The plaid green couch glinted in the sun, its rough fabric catching the light in strange ways. Rueben ran his hand across it, tracing the soft yellow and orange lines of the design. He'd always had a love-hate relationship with that couch. His parents had money—they could've replaced it a dozen times. But sentimentality won. It had belonged to his grandparents, and that made it sacred.

He sat down, sinking into the familiar stiffness, and watched the dust dance in the sunlight. It moved like it had purpose, like it was trying to tell him something.

He could almost see his father in the beige recliner, the indentations still etched into the cushion. The armrests were worn smooth from the dog that used to curl up beside him, tail thumping against the side.

The kidney bean-shaped coffee table sat in the center, scarred with rings from forgotten coasters—his fault, mostly.

Rueben stood and crossed the room.

The mantle was still painted forest green, matching the couch. The fireplace had long been boarded up, the old boxy TV now sitting in front of it like a tombstone.

Family photos lined the ledge.

Smiling faces.

Frozen moments.

Rueben stared at them, unsure if he was comforted or haunted.

Rueben stared at the photo—him and his parents at the beach, sunburned and smiling, sand clinging to their legs like glitter. His mother's arm was wrapped around his shoulder, her eyes squinting against the light.

And then it hit him.

She was dead.

This furniture shouldn't be here. This photo shouldn't be here. She shouldn't be here.

He whipped around, heart pounding, and stumbled forward. His foot caught on the raised edge of the gray carpet, the one that had curled up over years of foot traffic and neglect. He hit the floor hard, palms stinging, breath knocked from his chest.

Gathering himself, he pushed forward.

Toward the room.

Toward the memory.

"Mom?" he called out, voice thin, hesitant. It barely made it past his lips.

Silence.

Thick. Heavy. Wrong.

His stomach turned. Did he want to find her? Did he want to see her again, even like this?

His mind flashed—blood on the floor, the shattered lamp, the silence that followed.

None of this should be happening.

Then he heard it.

"In here," his mother's voice sang from the top of the stairs.

Sweet.

Familiar.

Terrifying.

He stood at the foot of the stairs, heart thudding in his chest.

Her voice had come from above.

Sweet. Familiar. Impossible.

His feet felt heavy, like the carpet had grown roots around his ankles.

He didn't know if he wanted to see her.

Or if he could survive it.

Rueben suddenly felt a strange sense of relief.

It didn't make sense.

Maybe it was the idea of seeing her again—his mother, whole and alive, not the broken image that haunted his sleep. Since the day Silas had taken her from him, Rueben's dreams had been nothing but blood and silence. This felt different. Softer. Warmer.

But that warmth was laced with fear.

Would this be another nightmare?

Would he open the door and find her there again—sprawled on the floor, eyes wide, the lamp glowing green beside her?

He was at the top of the stairs now.

The door to his parents' room stood just to the right.

It looked impossibly far away, though it was only a few steps. Like the hallway had stretched, like the house itself was resisting him.

Rueben reached out.

His hand trembled.

The door seemed to pulse, in sync with the blood rushing to his head. It shimmered slightly, like it was breathing.

He placed his hand on the knob.

Cold.

Metallic.

Familiar.

He turned it slowly, the click of the latch echoing louder than it should.

Then he pushed the door open.

And stepped inside.

The room was awash in light.

A soft breeze drifted through the open window, brushing Rueben's cheek like a whisper. The scent of lavender filled the air—clean, floral, familiar. His mother had always added lavender oil to the laundry, insisting it kept everything fresh for weeks. Rueben had never questioned it. He'd just loved it.

His heart flipped.

She was standing there.

Her dark hair cascaded down her shoulders, catching the sunlight in soft waves. The glow from the window framed her like something divine—an angel, maybe. Or a memory too perfect to be real.

She smiled.

And Rueben melted.

He rushed across the room, arms outstretched, and wrapped her in a hug. Her body was warm, solid, real. The scent of her perfume enveloped him—sandalwood, vanilla, and something else he couldn't name but had always known.

He gripped her shoulders, maybe too tightly, but he didn't care.

He couldn't let go.

Not yet.

Not again.

Her arms folded around him, gentle and steady, and for a moment Rueben felt like a child again—safe, whole, untouched by the Trials or the blood or the guilt.

He buried his face in her shoulder.

And breathed.

Reluctantly, Rueben pulled away and looked into her eyes.

They were brown, flecked with gold—tiny rivers of light that shimmered when she smiled. He'd always loved that about her. Those flecks had made her eyes feel warm, like sunlight through amber.

But then her gaze shifted.

Just for a second.

To the corner of the room.

Rueben turned instinctively, heart skipping, unsure what he expected to see.

Nothing.

Just the same soft light, the same lavender breeze, the same quiet.

He turned back.

Her smile hadn't changed.

Still gentle.

Still perfect.

Too perfect.

Something in his chest tightened.

"Do you mind running downstairs and grabbing me a glass of water?" she asked, her voice light, almost musical. Her hand grazed his elbow—soft, familiar, grounding.

Rueben hesitated.

"Sure," he said, though the word felt strange in his mouth.

He turned toward the door, casting one last glance over his shoulder.

She was still smiling.

Still glowing.

Still watching.

Rueben made his way toward the kitchen, each step slow, deliberate.

But before he reached the hallway, he turned back.

He had to.

She was still standing there, awash in sunlight, her smile soft and unwavering. The breeze from the window played with her hair, lifting strands like they were dancing.

He wanted to remember her like this.

Not the way he'd found her.

Not with fear etched into her face, frozen in that final moment. Not with blood pooling beneath her, the lamp shattered, the silence screaming louder than any sound.

This—this glow, this peace—was better.

It was mercy.

Rueben lingered for a second longer, memorizing the curve of her smile, the way the light kissed her cheekbones, the scent of lavender still hanging in the air.

Then he turned away.

And walked toward the kitchen.

Carrying the weight of memory with every step.

His mind was swirling as he stepped into the kitchen.

It should've been familiar.

But it wasn't.

He scanned the room, trying to remember where his parents used to keep the glasses. The layout tugged at something deep in his memory, but it didn't match what he knew now. Rueben had remodeled this kitchen years ago—ripped out the old cabinets, replaced the linoleum floors, painted everything a cool bluish gray.

But this wasn't that kitchen.

Or maybe it was.

He was getting flashes of both at once—his modern design overlaid with the outdated wooden frames, the chipped countertops, the brass handles that never quite matched. It was like his mind couldn't decide which version was real.

He reached for the bluish gray cabinet where he should have stored the glasses.

But inside were plates and bowls, stacked neatly in a space that hadn't existed in years.

Rueben blinked.

Opened another cabinet.

Then another.

Each one was wrong.

Until finally, he found it.

The right one.

The glasses were there—tall, clear, slightly fogged from age.

He stared at them for a moment, unsure if he should touch them.

Unsure if they'd shatter the illusion.

Rueben pulled out a ridged glass with a handle—one of the old ones, thick and heavy, the kind that never broke no matter how many times it was dropped. A chill ran down his spine as his fingers wrapped around it. He glanced behind him.

The room was still empty.

Too quiet.

He shook his head, trying to clear the fog. He needed to focus. Just get the water. Just do the task.

He walked to the double basin sink, grabbed the metal spicket, and swiveled it to the side. The cold tap groaned as he turned it on, and the water rushed out, clear and steady.

He placed the glass beneath the stream.

And watched.

The water rose.

Reached the rim.

Spilled over.

But his hand didn't move.

He just stood there, staring, lost in the swirl of thoughts that pulled him under.

This couldn't be real.

He knew that.

But he wanted it to be.

He wanted to stay in this moment forever—doing small things for his mother, earning that smile of approval, basking in the quiet pride she always had for him.

He wanted this to be the truth.

And everything else—the blood, the Trials, the years of terror—to be the nightmare.

His hand felt suddenly warm.

Too warm.

Rueben glanced down—and gasped.

Blood.

Thick, dark, cascading from the faucet like a slow-moving river. It coated his fingers, pooled in the ridged glass, and overflowed onto the black-and-white tiled floor. The contrast was stark—red against white, horror against order.

He reared back, heart hammering, and the glass slipped from his hand.

It shattered instantly, the sound sharp and final.

The blood oozed across the checkered ground, glinting under the harsh kitchen light. It moved with purpose, curling around the shards like it knew exactly where to go.

"What's taking so long?" his mother's voice called from the top of the stairs.

Not gentle.

Not warm.

Annoyed.

Rueben faltered.

He scrambled for another glass, his hands trembling, and turned the faucet again—this time watching the water like it might betray him. It ran clear. Cold. Normal.

He filled the glass and turned to leave.

But something tugged at him.

He looked back.

The blood was gone.

Just a puddle of water.

Just broken glass.

Rueben stared at it, unsure if he'd imagined the whole thing.

Or if the house was hiding it from him.

Rueben was still off-kilter, but the need to please her anchored him. Even if she wasn't real. Even if this was all a dream stitched together by grief and guilt.

She was still smiling when he returned, standing in the exact spot he'd left her. Unmoving. Serene.

He handed her the glass, and a strange pang of guilt twisted in his chest. He didn't understand it—he'd done what she asked. He'd brought her water. That should've been enough.

She took the glass with graceful fingers, lifted it to her lips.

The sunlight caught it.

A flicker of blue.

Rueben's breath hitched.

Water wasn't blue.

The glass wasn't blue.

His heart dropped.

No.

No, no, no.

She sipped.

And Rueben froze.

It wasn't a glass.

It was the vial.

That vial.

The one he'd used to poison Silas.

The one that had ended everything.

Horror wrapped around him like ice.

She smiled as she drank.

Rueben swatted the vial from her hand, but it was too late.

Her eyes locked onto his—wide, confused, mouth agape as if she were about to speak. But no words came.

Just foam.

White and frothing at the corners of her lips, bubbling like poison made visible.

Rueben lunged forward, catching her as her knees buckled. His arms wrapped around her, desperate, trembling. Tears streamed down his face, hot and relentless, blurring his vision as he tried to hold her upright.

But his own legs gave out.

They collapsed together, a heap of grief and horror on the bedroom floor.

He cradled her head, whispering apologies, begging her to stay, to breathe, to fight.

But she was slipping.

Her body convulsed gently, her breath shallow, her eyes losing focus.

Rueben sobbed, rocking her in his arms, the weight of guilt crushing his chest.

He was watching his mother die.

Again.

And there was nothing he could do.

Not in this dream.

Not in real life.

Not ever.

"I love you," Rueben whispered, voice cracking. "I'm so sorry, Mom. I should've come home sooner that night."

He held her in his lap, arms wrapped around her trembling frame. Her body convulsed violently, blood spurting from her mouth, matting her hair in thick, dark strands. Rueben sobbed, rocking her gently, trying to soothe her even as she seized against him.

He couldn't stop it.

Couldn't undo it.

Couldn't wake up.

Her breath came in short, ragged bursts, each one weaker than the last. Then the blood stopped. A thin trail of clear liquid slid down her chin, catching the light like a tear.

Her body stilled.

Rueben froze.

He leaned down, pressing a kiss to her forehead, his lips trembling against her skin. She was still warm.

With shaking fingers, he reached up and gently closed her eyes.

The room was silent now.

No breeze.

No lavender.

Just Rueben.

And the weight of goodbye.

"It's all your fault," said an icy, distant voice behind him.

The sound was jagged—like nails on a chalkboard, scraping across Rueben's spine. His stomach turned, bile rising in his throat.

He turned slowly.

And his heart sank.

Silas Thorn stood in the doorway.

The man who had murdered his mother.

The man Rueben had killed.

But he wasn't gone.

Not here.

Not in this place.

Silas's face was pale, almost translucent, like he'd been drained of everything human. His eyes were hollow, black pits that seemed to absorb the light around them. Behind him, a red glow pulsed—casting his silhouette in a hellish hue, like he'd stepped out of some infernal threshold.

infernal threshold.

Rueben couldn't move.

Couldn't breathe.

Silas didn't blink.

Didn't smile.

He just stared.

"You did this," he said again, voice low and venomous.

Rueben's arms tightened around his mother's lifeless body.

The blood on her lips.

The foam.

The silence.

Silas took a step forward.

And the red light followed.

Suddenly, all the fear and grief drained from Rueben's body.

What filled him was rage.

Pure, blinding, righteous rage.

This man—this thing—was the reason his mother had died. Not Rueben. Not fate. Him.

He was going to get his revenge.

Again.

Rueben surged to his feet, heart pounding, legs trembling with adrenaline. He charged at Silas, fists clenched, teeth bared. If he could just reach him—just tackle him, shove him down the stairs, end it—maybe the dream would finally let him breathe.

But Silas vanished.

Gone.

No sound. No flash. No resistance.

Just absence.

Rueben stumbled forward, arms grasping at air, and then—

Everything dissolved.

The hallway. The stairs. The house.

Gone.

He was thrust into the void again.

Blinding white.

No floor beneath him.

No walls around him.

Just light.

And silence.

And the echo of his own scream, swallowed by the emptiness.

He squinted, desperate to find Silas in the blinding void.

But there was nothing.

Just white.

Just silence.

Then the voices returned—sharp, relentless, echoing through his skull.

You did this!

It's all your fault!

They grew louder, overlapping, crashing into each other until Rueben couldn't breathe. He clutched his head, trying to drown them out, but they were inside him now.

He let out a visceral scream.

And collapsed.

Thunk.

His eyes flew open.

The pain of hitting the floor snapped him back to reality

He was still in the room.

Still one of the Selected.

It had all been a dream.

He knew that.

But it didn't feel like one.

Rueben blinked, heart racing, and glanced around to see if anyone had noticed.

Hazel was standing over him.

Her face was tight with concern.

And Rueben choked back another scream.

Because her eyes looked just like his mother's.

9.

Confessions

Rueben ignored Hazel as he gathered himself off the floor.

His face burned with embarrassment. Falling out of bed was bad enough—but someone seeing it? That was worse. He didn't want to explain. Didn't want to be asked if he was okay. He wasn't.

He brushed past her, not meeting her eyes, and made his way to the sinks.

The smell hit him instantly.

Bleach.

Blood.

It clung to the air like a warning, sharp and metallic, and Rueben's stomach turned. He clenched his jaw and turned the knob, letting cold water rush over his hands. He wanted to splash it on his face, to wake himself up, but the image of Silas's blood—thick, dark, endless— froze him in place.

He couldn't do it.

Not yet.

A cold shower. That would help. Maybe.

The nightmare had been so vivid. Too vivid. It made him question everything. Despite all the murders, all the pain—who was he to decide Silas's fate?

But then again…

It had to be one of them.

And Silas had killed his mother.

His mother.

She flashed through his mind again—standing in the sunlight, smiling. Then dying. Then gone.

Rueben gripped the edge of the sink, knuckles white.

He couldn't shake it.

Not the dream.

Not the memory.

Not the guilt.

A tear rolled down Rueben's cheek as he grabbed a towel from the trunk at the foot of his bed. He didn't bother wiping it away. What was the point?

He turned on his heels—and nearly collided with Hazel.

Of course.

Why was she always there? Always watching, always pushing?

Her eyes were sharp, her voice low and clipped. "We need to talk," she whispered, pointing toward the wall of showers.

Rueben rolled his eyes. Of course she picked now. Of course she couldn't wait.

He didn't respond. Just started walking.

He had to go that way anyway. And there was nowhere to hide from her. Not in this place. Not in this moment.

"Let's get this over with," he muttered, voice flat, and disappeared behind the wall.

Hazel followed.

And Rueben braced himself—not for the water, but for whatever truth she was about to drop.

The lights above the showers were the only ones still glowing in their confined prison-cell of a room.

Earlier in the evening, the overheads had been dimmed to give the players their much-needed rest—rest they'd never truly get, not with the Trials looming like vultures. The dimmed lights cast a sickly green hue across the tiled walls, bathing the shower stalls in a haunting glow.

Each stall stood like a sentinel—equipped with a single metal showerhead and white curtains so stark they seemed to hum with reflected light. The green shimmer danced across the fabric, making the room feel less like a place to clean up and more like a surgical theater waiting for its next subject.

The shower closest to Hazel and Rueben was still dripping.

A slow, rhythmic tap.

Someone hadn't turned it off all the way.

The sound echoed in the silence between them, like a countdown.

Or a warning.

"Are your nightmares from the guilt?" Hazel said, her voice low and sharp.

No warning. No buildup.

Rueben winced.

The question hit harder than it should have. Maybe because it was true. Maybe because she said it like she already knew.

He stared at her for a moment, weighing the silence.

Should he tell her?

Should he admit what haunted him?

Every instinct screamed no. The Trials had taught him that trust was a liability. Information was currency. And Hazel was smart—too smart. Was she fishing for leverage? A confession she could twist later?

He hesitated.

Then sighed.

"The stress of the evening was just getting to me," he said, voice flat. "I couldn't sleep. Which I'm assuming is the same reason you're awake at this hour."

She glared at him for a moment before answering.

"I'm awake because I feel like you're the only reason Silas is dead," she said, her voice low, her eyes unreadable.

Rueben stiffened.

"So you just had to come and ask me then?" he replied, his tone like ice. "Look, I'm not saying I had anything to do with his death. But even if I did—he was a murderer. He could've killed any of us in our sleep."

Hazel didn't flinch.

She just stared.

Like she was trying to peel him open with her eyes.

Rueben felt a chill crawl up his spine. He remembered the gameshow like introductions—how she used to help hack systems for the FBI. How she'd cracked encrypted networks like they were puzzles. But what else had she learned while she was there?

Did she work with profilers?

Could she see through him?

Through the lie?

"Wrong is wrong," Hazel said, her voice tight. "We don't stoop to the levels of others just because it benefits us."

Her fists were clenched now, knuckles white.

Rueben could see it—she was really upset. Not just suspicious. Disappointed.

That stung more than he expected.

"So what are you going to do?" he snapped, trying to sound composed, but his voice betrayed him— shaking, thin. "Tell the others I did it on purpose? He drank the vial that was meant for me. They'll never believe you."

Hazel didn't respond right away.

She just stared at him, eyes sharp, calculating.

Rueben felt exposed.

Like she could see the guilt crawling under his skin. Like she already knew the truth and was just waiting for him to admit it.

He swallowed hard.

The silence between them stretched, thick with accusation.

And Rueben wasn't sure which version of himself she saw.

The survivor.

Or the killer.

Rueben knew she could tell the others if she wanted to.

And they'd believe her.

Tensions were high. Trust was thin. Survival was everything. If Hazel painted him as a killer, the rest would turn on him without hesitation. He could already see it— whispers in the dark, alliances forming, eyes watching him during the Trials.

Would they cut his Achilles when danger struck?

Leave him behind?

Rueben clenched his jaw.

He had to play this right. Keep his secrets close. This wasn't about guilt anymore—it was about survival. And he wasn't going to lose.

Hazel sighed, her fists unclenching.

"Look," she said, voice softer now. "I'm going to level with you. I have a secret too. But I need to know I can trust you. I think you'd be a good asset—and you could benefit from what I'm hiding. But I need the truth."

She looked him dead in the eye.

"Did you set Silas up?"

Rueben tried to imagine what Hazel could possibly be hiding that would benefit him.

Nothing came to mind.

She was smart, sure. Resourceful. But what could she possibly offer that would make trusting her worth the risk?

"Well," he said, voice low, "why don't you share first—and I'll decide if it's beneficial."

Hazel's expression shifted.

She wasn't just calculating now—she was conflicted. Rueben could see it in the way her jaw tightened, the way her eyes flicked toward the dripping showerhead like she needed something to anchor her.

She was debating.

Not just whether to tell him—but whether it was worth the fallout.

"Well," she said finally, voice hesitant, "you know how we all got welcome letters before the first trial?"

Rueben's heart started to pound.

"Yeah," he said, trying to sound casual.

But something in her tone told him this wasn't going to be casual at all.

Where was she going with this?

Did she know what his welcome letter had said?

She couldn't have.

Rueben had flushed it the moment he got the chance. He remembered sneaking away while the others were still scrubbing blood off the floor, their faces pale and silent. There was only one toilet—far side of the showers, tucked behind a rusted stall door. He'd announced he needed a minute, made sure no one followed, and destroyed the evidence.

No one saw.

No one could know.

Hazel fidgeted with her hands, eyes flicking toward the dripping showerhead.

"Well," she said, voice low, "I believe everyone had a different letter. One with clues about the Trials."

Rueben's pulse quickened.

She continued. "I looked at Silas's letter. His said to trust the smartest person in the room. Which I guess, to him, was the Game Master. Someone who could possibly get out of this mess."

Rueben swallowed hard.

So the letters weren't just ceremonial.

They were strategic.

And Hazel had seen more than she let on.

"That's not much of a secret," Rueben said, arms crossed. "I assumed everyone had different letters. The Masked are sneaky like that."

Hazel twirled a strand of hair around her finger, biting her lip.

"That wasn't the secret," she said softly.

Rueben sighed, irritation rising. "Out with it then."

Hazel hesitated, then leaned in slightly, her voice barely above a whisper.

"Well… my letter had some interesting information. It said: Play your cards right and more than one person can survive the Trials. One can be saved, and one can be changed."

Rueben blinked.

The words echoed in his mind, twisting into something darker.

Saved.

Changed.

What did that mean?

Was someone going to be rescued? Redeemed? Reprogrammed?

He stared at Hazel, searching her face for clues. But she looked just as lost—just as haunted.

Rueben's heart pounded.

Because if her letter was true, then the Trials weren't just about surviving.

They were about choosing.

And Rueben wasn't sure what kind of change he could survive.

Rueben's mouth dropped open.

He hadn't expected that.

The Trials were designed to fracture alliances, pit players against one another, and leave only one standing. That was the rule. The law. The promise.

But Hazel's revelation cracked something open.

More than one person can survive.

It wasn't just a twist—it was a lifeline.

For a moment, Rueben felt something swell in his chest. Hope. Real, tangible hope. If Hazel was telling the truth—if her letter was genuine—then maybe survival didn't have to mean solitude. Maybe he didn't have to become the monster the Trials wanted him to be.

Her hacking skills. His game master instincts.

Together, they might stand a chance.

But then the dread returned.

Heavy. Cold.

Because if he wanted Hazel's trust—if he wanted to be part of whatever plan she was building—he'd have to give something in return.

His secret.

The one he'd buried.

The one that could unravel everything.

Rueben clenched the towel tighter in his hands.

He wasn't sure if he was ready.

But the Trials didn't wait.

"That's… very interesting," Rueben said, voice trembling. "And something that's never been done before. I would know—I've studied every piece of footage I could find. Every Trial. Every outcome. I've never seen clear alliances. Not once."

He was shaking now.

Not from fear.

From possibility.

Hazel nodded, her expression unreadable. "We'd have to keep it a secret. The note was meant for my eyes only. That means I get to choose who I trust. Who I share it with."

She glanced over her shoulder, scanning the room. Everyone else was still asleep. Still unaware.

They were alone.

She turned back to him, eyes sharp.

"Alright then," she said. "Can I trust you?"

A pause.

Then the knife.

"Or are you as crazed as Silas?"

Rueben felt the words hit like a slap.

He wasn't sure which part stung more—the comparison, or the fact that he didn't have an answer.

Not yet.

Rueben took a deep breath and let the truth spill.

He told Hazel everything.

The clue in his letter. The moment he recognized Silas during the announcements. The night he found his mother—her body cold, her eyes open, the silence unbearable.

Hazel's posture shifted.

She'd started tense, arms crossed, jaw tight. But as Rueben spoke, her shoulders relaxed. Her eyes softened. She leaned in, listening—not calculating, but feeling.

When he got to the nightmare, the tears came.

He didn't try to stop them.

Hazel rubbed his back, awkward but sincere. Rueben could tell she wasn't used to emotions—especially not ones this raw. But she stayed. She didn't flinch.

He told her about watching his mother die again. About Silas haunting him in the dream. About the scream, the void, the guilt.

Hazel nodded, slowly.

Rueben could see it—she was beginning to see him. Not just a player. Not just a threat.

But then—

A shuffle.

Behind the wall.

Both of them froze.

The sound was soft, but unmistakable.

Someone was awake.

Someone had heard.

And Rueben's heart dropped.

Because secrets in the Trials were never safe.

Someone else was awake and they were headed in their direction. Hazel grabbed his wrist and pulled him into the shower behind them and silently slid the curtain closed.

Ivy shuffled by a few seconds later, rubbing her eyes and heading to the toilet. She did not even notice them huddled together in the shower, even though Rueben was certain that their feet could be seen despite the closed curtain.

A few moments later she shuffled back by and Rueben chanced a peek around the curtain. He could barely see Ivy round the corner again to head back to bed.

He turned back to look at Hazel. "Well? Partners?" he asked nervously as his voice cracked.

"Partners" she said and they both headed back to bed.

10.

Heating Up

The next morning bled into the afternoon with no announcement, no movement, no sign of the next Trial.

The silence was suffocating.

Tensions simmered beneath the surface, quiet but palpable.

Ivy sat curled in the corner, nibbling on a snack she'd stashed from breakfast. Her eyes darted around the room between bites, like she expected someone to snatch it from her hands.

Trinity was sprawled across her bed, one arm dangling off the edge, breathing slow and steady. Rueben wondered if she was actually asleep or just pretending—trying to escape the weight of waiting.

Hank was relacing his shoes for the third time. Rueben watched him loop and tighten, loop and tighten. Was it preparation? Or just something to do to keep his hands busy?

Victor grunted through a set of push-ups near the doorway, sweat dripping from his nose onto the concrete.

Rueben frowned.

Would Victor have anything left if the Trial started now?

Or was this his way of staying sharp—burning off fear before it could settle?

Rueben and Hazel had been avoiding each other since last night.

No words. No glances.

Just silence.

They'd agreed—without saying it—that their alliance would stay hidden. Rueben watched her from across the room as she sat on her bed, braiding and unbraiding her hair in a loop that felt more like a coping mechanism than a style choice.

He sat stiffly on his own bed, eyes scanning the others.

Ivy, curled in the corner, nibbling on her stolen snack.

Trinity, napping with one arm flung over her face.

Hank, relacing his shoes with obsessive precision.

Victor, grunting through push-ups, sweat pooling beneath him.

Rueben wasn't sure if they were preparing for something—or just trying to stay sane.

Then the intercom crackled to life.

"GOOD EVENING, SELECTED," it boomed, sterile and sharp.

Everyone jolted.

"PLEASE LINE UP AT THE DOOR. YOU WILL BE ESCORTED TO DINNER."

The room shifted.

Stillness replaced by movement.

And Rueben felt the dread return.

The group shuffled into line behind Victor, who wiped the sweat from his brow like he'd just finished a marathon. Natalie came sprinting around the corner from the bathroom, breathless, and slipped into place ahead of Rueben. He let her pass without a word, falling to the back just as the door creaked open.

Eight Masked figures entered.

Each one massive. Each one silent.

They moved with mechanical precision, their faces hidden behind identical black masks. One Masked per Selected—except Victor.

Victor got two.

Rueben's eyes narrowed.

So they were afraid of him. Afraid he might snap, might overpower one of them if given the chance. That was good to know. If things ever went south with Hazel, maybe Victor could be useful.

But Rueben shook his head.

No.

Victor was too self-centered. Too volatile. He didn't play well with others—he played for himself.

And Rueben couldn't afford to bet on a wildcard.

Not now.

Rueben couldn't shake the feeling of dread in his stomach.

It wasn't just nerves—it felt like his guts were tying themselves into knots, twisting tighter with every step toward the hallway. He swallowed hard, trying to keep the nausea down.

Something was wrong.

They were leaving the room for dinner.

That had never happened before.

Breakfast had been served right here—laid out buffet-style across the long metal table. Eggs, bacon, grits, cereal bars. Surprisingly good, considering the circumstances. The Selected had scattered to eat in corners, on beds, anywhere they could find space. The Masked had stood watch, silent and looming, making sure every piece of silverware was returned. No weapons. No exceptions.

But lunch never came.

Rueben hadn't noticed it at first. Too distracted. Too tired. But now, as his stomach growled beneath the dread, it hit him.

They were being starved.

Not just physically.

Strategically.

And now they were being moved.

Which meant something was coming.

Something worse than breakfast.

The hallway was unnaturally clean.

Fluorescent lights buzzed overhead, casting a sterile glow on the white-painted cement walls. Rueben reached out, dragging his fingers along the ruts in the surface— tiny imperfections that reminded him of school hallways. The memory was fleeting, but it made the place feel even more surreal.

Doors lined both sides of the corridor, each one identical, each equipped with a card reader that blinked red.

Rueben's eyes drifted to the badge clipped to his escort's side. It swung with each step, catching the light. He squinted, trying to read the clearance level and the barcode numbers trailing beneath it. No photo. No name.

Just a void.

Preserving anonymity.

Why go to such lengths?

Rueben had always assumed the Masked weren't human. Not really. Not after the ship. Not after the way they moved. But then why not add a name unless they were human after all.

Were they still on the ship?

Rueben had his doubts.

The vessel they arrived on was massive—easily the size of Madison Square Garden. Big enough to house dozens of rooms like the one they'd been confined to. But something didn't sit right.

The walls were bricked.

Concrete. Cement. Heavy materials that didn't belong on a ship meant to fly.

So they had to be in some sort of facility

Ruebens stomach twisted as he decided that they had to have been housed somewhere in the middle of nowhere. Some place in an undisclosed location away from the prying eyes of the government. Was it hidden underground or built into the side of a mountain? It had to be in order for them to stay out of site to any overhead planes.

A place designed for containment. For control. For disposal.

The layout, the silence, the sterile corridors—it all pointed to something darker. Somewhere underground, since there were no windows. Somewhere they could get rid of bodies without anyone asking questions.

Rueben swallowed hard.

This wasn't just a game.

It was a system.

And he was inside it.

His thoughts were interrupted as they rounded the corner into the dining room.

It was massive.

A long wooden table dominated the center, its surface gleaming with a red-tinted glow that could only come from cherry wood polished to perfection. Rueben's eyes traced the grain, hypnotized for a moment by the way it caught the light.

Above, chandeliers hung in a perfect line—one after another, spiraling like twisted helixes. They emitted a soft red hue, casting the room in a strange warmth that felt more like blood than comfort.

Seven placements were arranged along the table, each one spaced unevenly, as if chosen with intention. Fine china sat pristine in front of high-backed wooden chairs, and the silverware shimmered under the red light, scattering tiny flecks of crimson across the room like shattered rubies.

Rueben's stomach turned.

This wasn't just dinner.

It was a performance.

And they were the cast.

The wooden chairs were spread out evenly across the table. Three chairs lined each side of the table. One chair was strategically placed at the head of the table farthest from the door.

The booming voice came over the intercom telling everyone to take their seats and to pay special attention to the engravings on the chairs.

That is when Rueben noticed that the chairs had names engraved into the backs across the piece of wood that ran along the top of the head rest.

The group started around the table to find their seats. Victor, Hank, and Trinity all sat along the left side of the table. Victor sat down very nonchalant, like he did not have much of a care in the world. Hank and Trinity both seemed a little nervous as they looked around the room searching for signs of danger. Rueben doesn't blame them for it, something was making him feel uneasy as well. He wiped the sweat from his brow as he watched the others take their seats.

Hazel, Ivy, and Natalie sat on the right side of the table in sucession with one another. Hazel was closest to the head of the table and she sat down after investigating every inch of the chair, looking for anything that might harm her. Seeing that the chair was safe, she took her seat. Ivy threw her chair back and sat down with confidence, all while glaring at the Masked who had lead us into the room. Natalie sat closest to the door and across from Victor. She tried offering him a wry smile and was promptly ignored.

That left the seat at the head of the table. Rueben wiped the sweat of his palms as he looked at the ornate carving of his name on the seat that was placed all alone. He did not like that he was going to have to sit here and watch everyone, but that also meant he could study their movements and figure out where the competition lies. He attempted to look at Hazel but then he realized that everyone was watching him take his seat and he gulped down the lump in his throat and he scraped the chair back. The chair felt a little damp and he could feel the moisture seep through his pants as he sat. Was it hot in here or was he just nervous cause he was the center of attention?

The chair scraped loudly against the floor, the sound sharp and jarring in the otherwise hushed room.

Rueben winced.

He lowered himself into the seat, the dampness soaking through his pants like a warning. It clung to him, cold and clammy, and he couldn't tell if it was sweat or something else. Something left behind.

He glanced toward Hazel, hoping for reassurance, but she was staring straight ahead, her expression unreadable.

Everyone else was watching him.

Not just looking—calculating. Measuring. Interpreting.

Rueben forced a sheepish grin, then pointed toward the door like it meant something. Attempting a distraction. Like it could shift the attention away from him.

It didn't.

The chandeliers above spiraled slowly, casting red shadows across the table.

Rueben swallowed hard.

This seat wasn't just symbolic.

It was a spotlight.

And he was trapped in it.

He sheepishly nodded at all of them and pointed to the door again, trying to force them to look away. Again it didn't work.

The Masked that had led us in the room started to file out, and returned a moment later with platters of food. It was a massive spread of food that reminded Rueben of Thanksgiving dinner. There was turkey and dressing, mashed potatoes and macaroni and cheese, green bean casserole, and yams. As everything began to get placed on the table, an announcement was made for us to help ourselves and don't be shy.

Victor was the first one to make a move, shoveling food onto his plate. Hank followed suit right after, taking massive portions. Rueben watched as his stomach rumbled. He would not be the first one to eat. What if this was a trial and some of the food was poisoned? He did not think they would poison people in two trials but it would better be safe than sorry.

Rueben's stomach growled again, louder this time.

Victor was already halfway through his plate, chewing with open defiance. Hank followed suit, scooping mashed potatoes like he hadn't eaten in days. Trinity hesitated, then reached for the green bean casserole, her hand trembling slightly.

Rueben stayed still.

The food looked perfect. Too perfect. Steam curled from the turkey, the macaroni glistened under the red chandelier light, and the yams were dusted with cinnamon like someone had cared.

But Rueben knew better.

This wasn't care.

It was deception.

He scanned the table, watching for signs—a cough, a wince, a sudden collapse. Nothing yet.

Hazel hadn't moved either. She was watching the others, just like him.

Rueben met her eyes for a brief second.

No words.

Just shared caution.

He reached for a roll, slowly.

If this was a test, he'd play it safe. He forced a bite.

Rueben took another bite, slower this time.

Seeing that it was safe, he added more food to his plate.

The macaroni melted on his tongue, rich and familiar. The mashed potatoes, smooth and warm beneath the gravy, reminded him of comfort—of home. Of the way his mom used to hum while stirring the pot, the way his dad would sneak extra rolls when he thought no one was looking.

He glanced around the table.

Everyone was eating now. Even Hazel, though she still scanned the room between bites. Ivy had her feet propped up on the chair beside her, chewing with theatrical confidence. Natalie pushed Ivy's feet off the arm rest with a disgusted look. Victor was already halfway through his second plate.

Rueben wondered—had the others before them eaten like this?

Or had they been fed slop and silence?

Was this feast a reward?

Or a setup?

He swallowed hard, the warmth of the food suddenly heavier in his stomach.

Because in the Trials, comfort was never free.

And nostalgia could be a trap.

After eating until he thought he might puke, Rueben leaned back in his chair and sighed. The food was good, but he couldn't help but feel as if something was wrong. He glanced around to see that everyone else was slowing down on the food as well. Hazel was wiping her neck with her napkin, trying to get the sweat off the back of her hairline. Trinity was chugging water like she had just run a marathon in the Sahara. Hank was running his hands across his pants attempting to dry them off.

"I HOPE YOU ALL ENJOYED YOUR MEAL, NOW TIME FOR DESSERT." the voice boomed from overhead, giving everyone a startle. "REVENGE IS A DISH BEST SERVED, SWEET. SOMEONE IN THIS GROUP HAD KNOWLEDGE OF THE POISON

FROM THE PREVIOUS TRIAL. THIS TRAITOR HAD THE INTENTIONS OF OFFING ONE OF YOU. RETURN THAT FAVOR AND SACRIFICE THEM BEFORE THINGS COME TO A BOIL"

Rueben's stomach twisted.

The food sat heavy now, no longer comforting—just wrong. His mouth went dry as he scanned the table.

Hazel had stopped wiping her neck. She was frozen, eyes locked on the chandelier above, as if waiting for it to drop.

Trinity's water glass trembled in her hand.

Hank looked pale, his fingers twitching against his pants.

Victor was still chewing, slower now, eyes narrowed like he was calculating odds.

Rueben's heart pounded.

Someone was trying to out him for the poison.

The voice hadn't said who, but who else could it have been.

Because Rueben had the clue.

And Hazel knew.

He glanced at her, just once.

She didn't look back.

The intercom crackled again.

"YOU HAVE FIVE MINUTES TO DECIDE. THE TRAITOR MUST BE CHOSEN. IF NO DECISION IS MADE, THE ROOM WILL DECIDE FOR YOU."

Rueben felt the sweat bead at his temples.

This wasn't just a test.

It was a purge.

And he was at the head of the table, getting all of the attention.

Rueben's breath caught in his throat, threatening to cut off his oxygen. Sweat was building up on his forehead and starts to drip down his face. He froze. Any form of movement would attract the attention of the others. The bead of sweat burned as it grazed the corner of his eye. It trailed slowly down at an angle, tickling the tip of his nose. His eyes crossed as he tried to look at the droplet that was trying to sabotage his composure. He watched as it slipped into his glass, which now seemed to be sweating just as much as he was.

The rest of the group was silent. Everyone seemed to be looking around the room at one another trying to assess which of their peers had been a traitor.

The silence was suffocating.

No one spoke. No one moved.

Rueben could hear the faint hum of the chandeliers above, the soft clink of silverware as someone adjusted their grip. But mostly, it was the sound of silence—the quiet calculation of seven minds trying to pinpoint a threat.

Hazel's eyes flicked toward him, just once.

Not accusing.

Not forgiving.

Just a glance of acknowledgment.

Victor leaned back in his chair, arms crossed, chewing slowly like he was waiting for someone to crack. Ivy tapped her fingers against her plate, rhythm steady, gaze sharp. Trinity looked pale, her water glass empty, her lips pressed into a thin line.

Rueben's heart thudded against his ribs.

He felt like a bug under glass.

The bead of sweat in his cup had vanished now, swallowed by the water. But its trail still burned on his skin.

He wanted to speak.

To explain.

To confess.

But the room wasn't ready for the truth.

It was hungry for blood.

"It had to have been Rueben, he was the one that told Silas about the blue vial." Trinity was the first to speak.

"Of course she would be the one to point the finger." Rueben thought to himself as he looked at her in shock. The cop would put the pieces together before anyone else.

Rueben chanced a glance at Hazel who had a look of determination on her face. Would this be where she betrays him and confirms it to the group that he was the one who killed Silas?

"If you remember correctly, he was about to drink that vial himself." said Hazel.

"Exactly, that very well could have been me writhing on the floor." Rueben said, grateful Hazel had stepped in. He turned back toward Trinity who was now clenching her knife in her hand.

"He is a game master for the best escape room in the city though, he could have figured it out and tricked Silas." said Victor.

Rueben felt a lump form into his chest. This was not going the way that he had planned. This could be the last trial for him. He could be dead by the end of the evening, and he couldn't help but think that maybe he did deserve it. Even if his actions were justified, he still was the cause of someone else's demise.

Rueben felt the lump in his chest start to harden.

It wasn't just fear anymore.

It was guilt.

Heavy. Unrelenting.

Victor's words echoed in his head—*he could have figured it out and tricked Silas*. And maybe he had. Maybe not intentionally. Maybe not maliciously. But the result was the same.

Silas was dead.

And Rueben had lived.

Trinity's grip on the knife tightened, her knuckles pale. Hazel remained still, her defense hanging in the air like a fragile thread. Rueben wanted to thank her, but the words wouldn't come. Not with everyone watching. Not with the weight of judgment pressing down on him like a vice.

He glanced at the chandelier above, its spiral casting red shadows across the table.

This could be it.

His final Trial.

And maybe he deserved it.

Even if his actions were justified—even if Silas was dangerous—Rueben had still played a part in someone's death.

And now the room was deciding whether that part was enough to end him.

"Yeah, he would be our greatest competition in the trials. He does shit like this for a living and could go all the way if we don't take him out now." Hank agreed, getting up from his chair.

Rueben stumbled backward out of his chair, attempting to get away from the mob forming in front of him.

"That might be why he was seated at the head of the table" said Trinity.

"We had assigned seats, and we have an uneven amount of people, it could have been any of you" he responded, his voice cracking.

"Trinity was the first one to point a finger, maybe she is trying to deflect. She could have been the one that knew." Hazel interjected again.

Rueben half smiled at her as he wondered what the group might think.

"Like Hank said, he is still the biggest competition. I say we take him out regardless. Then we can move on." Victor chimed in.

"He could also be our greatest asset and potentially help more people survive," said Natalie who nodded slightly in his direction.

Rueben's back hit the wall behind his chair.

He steadied himself, heart pounding, eyes darting between the faces now turning on him. Hank was still standing, fists clenched. Trinity's knife gleamed under the red chandelier light. Victor leaned forward, elbows on the table, like he was watching a game unfold.

Hazel hadn't moved.

Natalie's nod gave him a flicker of hope.

He swallowed hard.

"I didn't trick Silas," he said, voice low. "I didn't plan it. I didn't want it. But I did survive. And if that makes me dangerous, then maybe you should ask yourselves why survival feels like a threat."

The room was silent.

Rueben could feel the weight of their stares pressing into him, each one calculating, deciding.

He wasn't sure if they saw a traitor.

Or a martyr.

And he wasn't sure which was worse.

Rueben was really sweating now as he glanced around the room. He was only seeing red. The anger, guilt and fear he was feeling was making him reach his breaking point. He was fumbling trying to find the right words that could save his life, when Ivy got up and started pacing the room. The next words out of her mouth hit Rueben right in the gut as she dropped a bombshell. The room began to spin as he registered the magnitude of her confession.

"Rueben killed Silas. I heard him and Hazel talking about it last night in the showers."

Rueben's breath caught.

The room tilted.

Ivy's words echoed like a gunshot, ricocheting off the walls and lodging deep in his chest.

Rueben killed Silas.

The accusation hung in the air, thick and suffocating. Rueben's vision blurred at the edges, the red haze intensifying until it felt like the chandeliers themselves were bleeding.

He opened his mouth, but no words came.

Hazel's face was unreadable.

Victor leaned forward some more, eyes sharp.

Trinity gripped her knife even more, knuckles turning white.

Hank took a step closer.

Rueben tried to push back even further, as if he was trying to fuse himself with the chair. The silence was no longer tense—it was charged. Like the room itself was waiting for a verdict.

"Ivy," Hazel said slowly, voice low, "how much of that conversation did you hear?"

Ivy didn't flinch. "I was on the way to the bathroom, when I heard the whispers. I heard enough."

Rueben's heart pounded.

This wasn't just a trial.

It was an execution.

And the blade was already swinging.

11.

Boiling Point

Rueben was still trying to process the impact of the confession that Ivy had just released upon the group, when a flash of movement caught his eye.

Victor was climbing up onto the table making the cherry wood groan underneath his weight. Victor ran straight at Rueben, glasses shattering, plates cracking as he made his way across the long wooden slab separating them.

Rueben tried to move, but was too slow.

His body tensed as bodies slammed and wood splintered.

He could feel the air leaving his body as Victor laid on top of him, with the chair in pieces below him. Hot, warm liquid was gushing down the side of his body. Looking down he saw a sharp piece of wood sticking out just below his ribcage.

Rueben gasped, but no air came.

Victor's weight pressed down like a slab of concrete, crushing his lungs, grinding the broken chair into his back. The sharp wood jutting from his side pulsed with every heartbeat, each throb a cruel reminder that he was still alive—for now.

The room spun.

Red light from the chandeliers danced across shattered china and spilled gravy, painting the scene like a massacre. Rueben's fingers twitched, reaching instinctively for the wound, but stopped short. Touching it might make it real.

Victor didn't move.

Hazel was shouting—he thought. Or maybe it was Ivy. Or maybe the intercom had come back to life.

Rueben couldn't tell.

His ears were ringing, his vision tunneling. The warmth down his side was turning sticky, cold. He blinked, trying to focus, trying to stay conscious.

Looking back up he could see the rage in Victors eyes. He gasped for air as he felt his rough calloused hands wrap around his neck.

"You murderous scumbag," Victor said through clenched teeth.

Rueben felt Victor's grip tighten as his nails dug into his neck. It was getting difficult to breathe and the pain in his side wasn't helping. He started to see stars as Victor leaned in closer to his ear.

"I've seen some pretty terrible things overseas, but even then we allowed most of our targets to live. We gave them a chance to redeem themselves or to give up valuable information. YOU took that away from him. You are just as evil and sadistic as he was. The only difference is that you hide your crazy better than he did."

Rueben clawed at Victor's wrists, but his strength was fading.

The stars in his vision multiplied, swirling like galaxies behind his eyelids. His lungs screamed for air, his side throbbed with every heartbeat, and the wood beneath him felt like it was sinking into his spine.

Victor's breath was hot against his ear, his words venomous.

Rueben wanted to speak. To explain. To fight back.

But all he could do was gasp.

He wasn't sure if the tears streaming down his face were from pain, fear, or the weight of Victor's accusation. Maybe all three.

He wasn't a monster.

Was he?

He'd tried to survive. Tried to protect everyone. Tried to make sense of chaos.

But now, pinned beneath fury and splinters, Rueben felt something crack—not just in his ribs, but in his resolve.

If this was how it ended—

He needed someone to see him.

Not as a killer.

But as a boy who never asked to play this game.

However, Rueben couldn't help but to feel guilty. Was what he said true? Was he just as bad? Or was this lack of oxygen getting to him? He tried to look for anything that could help him, a fork or glass, something that he could use as a weapon. Everything was blurred and his field of view was small due to the meaty fingers holding his throat closed.

That is when it hit him.

He had a weapon, and it was currently sticking out of his side.

Without a second thought he grabbed the splinter of wood and yanked it out of his side.

Tears stung his eyes, and he could hear a sickening pop and the squelching of his blood.

He then took the stake that he now brandished and jabbed it quickly into Victor's thigh.

Victor roared in pain, trying to keep his grip around Ruebens throat. Rueben shifted his weight and brought his knee up right into Victor's groin.

Air flooded his lungs, and for a brief moment, the world sharpened. His chest burned, but he was alive.

He stumbled as he gathered his footing, trying to get up and put as much distance between him and Victor as he could. He glanced over to see that Hazel was looking at him concerned. He gave her a slight nod to motion that he was ok, and her shoulders seemed to sag in relief. He turned back to face the rest of the group just to see Hank barreling toward him. He barely stepped out of the way before Hank smashed into the wall behind him.

Panting and heaving Rueben grabbed the chair with Ivy's name on it and backed himself into the corner trying to protect himself from anymore attacks. Hank was turning around now with blood dripping from his nose mixing with the sweat glistening off his chin. His chest was heaving as he tried to catch his breath. Victor was grunting and trying to get the stake out of his leg. Rueben's lungs burned as he gasped, the air thick and heavy, carrying the bitter scent of sweat and blood. His grip tightened around the chair's splintered edges, the wood cutting into his palm—but right now, pain was the least of his concerns.

"Can I have a chance to explain myself?" Rueben asked the group even though his voice was shaking.

"If you knew why he did it, then you guys might be willing to turn a blind eye, and we can all try and work together to get out of this room." Hazel chimed in while wiping sweat from her brow.

He was trying to catch his breath, but the air felt too thick. Rueben realized then just how warm it was in the room. The temperature had to have risen at least ten to twelve degrees since the start of dinner.

"One minute," said Ivy. Her face was lacking any emotion, and it was hard for Rueben to discern her reaction. "You have one minute to convince us you deserve to live."

Rueben couldn't think clearly with all the pressure that seemed to be building in his head.

He had one minute to impress these people and convince them that he was worthy of living.

Would telling them the truth even matter?

They could still see him as a threat if they knew that he was making the trials personal.

The heat was beginning to become unbearable and that is when Rueben saw it.

The circular chandeliers hanging over the tables were glowing a brighter red and he could see the stain on the chairs starting to bubble ever so slightly.

It seemed that everyone in the room was sweating, and it was not due to the *exciting* turn of events.

Could he use this to his advantage?

If the group saw that the room was becoming more dangerous would that help him or make things worse? They could just kill him faster if they thought it would save them. The sweat was running down into the cut on his leg causing him to wince in pain.

"Thirty seconds" Ivy said with a hint of annoyance in her voice.

Rueben still didn't know if it was worth spilling his secret. The pain was almost too much to bear and with the rising tensions in the room it might not even matter. He could just blame it on how psychotic Silas was. That he was taking out the most dangerous player to save everyone else. That would make him seem like a team player. He was running out of time, and he did not know what to do. How would everyone react? He did not want the pity of the group; he just wanted to survive the games and get out of here.

"Ten seconds" said Victor, now holding the stake from his leg. It was dripping with blood, causing a puddle to form between them.

"Fuck this, I'll tell them since you are too chicken shit." Hazel said forcing Rueben out of his thoughts.

"Silas was a deranged maniac who killed Rueben's mother. Rueben was trying to protect all of us here by taking out the real monster in the group. Now if we could all just work together and stop fighting, then maybe we could find a way out of here. In case none of you have noticed, these lovely chandeliers are heating the room up like an oven and we will all die if we don't come up with a solution."

Rueben stood there in the deafening silence that followed Hazel's outburst.

He could hear his blood rushing and feel the blood oozing out of his abdomen forcing his shirt to stick to the wound like glue.

Ivy glanced at him with regret all over her face, causing Rueben to wonder if she was feeling sorry for him now.

It would help to have someone else in his corner.

The room was almost now completely awash in a red haze, and Rueben could not tell if the hue of the room or the intense heat was causing his vision to blur, or maybe it was the blood still oozing out of his body.

Victor still had not moved, but his grip had loosened slightly on the stake forcing it to sway back and forth making the blood fly off in tendrils. Trinity was trying not to make eye contact with him and he didn't quite blame her really. The entire room was ready to sacrifice him just to save their own skin.

He looked over to Hank and saw the pale ashen look painted across his face. He was no longer sweating and he looked as though he may have seen a ghost.

With no warning at all, Hank collapsed to the ground in a heap next to the crimson pool of blood.

Natalie let out a little scream, and Victor rushed to Hank's side finally letting go of the stake.

"Get me some water and a towel or something" Victor screamed. There was not a single waver in his voice as his military training took over.

This was Ruebens' chance to get back in the good graces of the group. He set down the chair and quickly grabbed the water pitcher that the Masked had brought in just before the dinner was served. It was hot to the touch and Rueben screamed out in pain as the metal container clanged off the floor, the sound reverberating off the walls.

"You fucking idiot," Victor scowled. "Hazel, do you mind?"

Hazel crossed the room to grab the other pitcher, wrapping her hand in her shirt before taking hold of the handle.

Victor took the pitcher and poured water into a glass.

"The water is to keep you hydrated, we can't do anything to cool you down. The room is heating up too quickly" he said as he reached to the table behind him and grabbed a straw. "Take small sips, if you drink too much you can pass out, especially since the water is not cool."

Trinity is at his side now and she has a knife in her hand. For a moment Rueben thinks that she is about to take Hank out of his misery, and he let out a small gasp. To his relief she makes a small incision on his shirt and then rips the fabric off his body.

His body is covered in red bumps, and it looks as if the skin is boiling underneath the surface. Hank tries to sit up and falls back down onto his back huffing as he hits the hard ground.

He rolls over to his side and yanks the glass out of Victors hand with the last bit of strength he can muster and starts to drink ferociously.

"Stop it you old fool, you are going to kill yourself" Ivy says with a sharp intensity.

No sooner than the words leave her mouth and Hanks' eyes roll to the back of his head and he falls back making a sickening crack on the cement.

Victor and Trinity both reach up for the soft side of his neck to feel for a pulse. Making eye contact they shake their heads and drop their hands.

"He's gone" said Trinity as she grabs the shredded pieces of his shirt to cover his head.

The room is again engulfed in a treacherous silence. The chandeliers above humming as they continue to heat up the room.

"HE'S DEAD! THIS IS WHAT YOU WANTED ISN'T IT? LET THE REST OF US GO!" Hazel screams as tears start to gush down her face. She is walking straight toward the Masked in the corner of the room.

She gets right up in the face of one of the big brutes. "Let us go" she whimpers trying to regain her composure.

For a long moment he doesn't move and Rueben begins to wonder if he might also be dead. Or maybe he just doesn't care. He has probably seen a lot of people die from behind the safety of that mask and is now desensitized to all of the gruesome events that unfold.

Finally, he nods.

It was the smallest of movements, and Rueben almost did not register it.

With a loud click the door to the room swung open letting in a cool breeze.

The soft glow of the chandeliers started to diminish and the room immediately felt ten times better than before.

Rueben let out a sigh of relief, he had survived another trial. It was not how he planned for it to go, but now he was one step closer to getting out of there.

12.

The Plan

The walk back to the room was silent. Rueben's footsteps were echoing in his head, reverberating off of his skull. Blood trailed along behind him as it continued to drip from his body.

The group had not made a sound as they all trailed back to their cell. The soft glow of the fluorescent lights made Rueben feel slightly at peace.

He did not realize how tense that trial had made him. Taking in a deep breath and slowly letting it out he let his shoulders finally sag.

For some reason the Masked had led them in a different direction on the way back. Rueben assumed that this was so that they could not formulate an escape plan. They were passing hallway after hallway, taking turn after turn. He had tried to keep up in the beginning, but now his legs were burning and he could barely catch his breath. Why were they walking so long and how big was this place? Were they walking in circles? Everything looked the same with rows of doors along the white brick.

They passed another hallway on the left and Rueben made awkward eye contact with the Masked brute. He was standing in front of a doorway three doors down and he was watching the group intently, ensuring we all kept moving and did not start in his direction.

Rueben felt uneasy at seeing the guard. What was behind that door? What else on this ship needed to be guarded other than them? Were there two groups this time or was there something more sinister there?

Rueben slowed his pace just slightly, enough to glance back without drawing attention.

The Masked didn't move.

But his head tilted—just a fraction—as if acknowledging Rueben's curiosity. Or warning him.

The door behind him was unmarked. No number. No symbol. Just a slab of metal embedded in white brick, like it had been sealed shut for years. Rueben's stomach twisted.

What was in there?

Another group?

A failed experiment?

Or something worse—something not meant to be seen.

Hazel brushed past him, her shoulder grazing his arm. "Don't stare," she whispered, barely audible. "They notice."

Rueben nodded, eyes forward again.

But the image of that door stayed with him.

And the brute guarding it.

Because if they were the ones being tested…

Then what the hell was that being protected?

Rueben shook his head trying to shake off any feeling as he tried to memorize the route again.

He took a deep shuddering breath as he clenched his side in pain, and forced himself to keep moving.

The building was truly a maze of hallways, designed to keep you trapped if you were to try and escape. He did not know if they were walking in circles or not due to every hallway looking the exact same, making him wonder if he was just losing his mind on the walk back.

By the time that Rueben and the gang made it back to the room they were all out of breath and shuffling through the door like they had just ran a marathon. He showered as quickly as he could due to the pain in his legs and then collapsed onto his bed making the plastic on the mattress crinkle.

***

He awoke in a cold sweat and was trying to catch his breath.

He did not even remember falling asleep.

Clearing the gunk from his eyes he looked around and had to stifle a scream.

Hazel was standing at the foot of his bed staring down at him.

Again.

"What the fuck are you doing?" he asked in a harsh whisper.

"I was about to wake you, I noticed you thrashing around in your sleep and was going to check on you" she said as she glanced around the room. "Come on we need to talk anyway."

He sighed and put his feet to the cold floor. He followed Hazel around to the showers and they walked all the way down to the end and went into the stall they had the night before.

The tiles in the stall were white, save for the slight yellow tinge that circled the drain in the floor. A few tiles were loose underneath his footing as they went to the far wall to sit underneath the showerhead.

How old was this place? He sat down and looked to Hazel putting all previous thoughts to rest.

He chanced a glance at his side and noticed that it was stitched up and patched. They must have done it in his sleep.

"Did you notice that guard in front of the door on the way back?" she asked stealing his attention back to her.

"How could I not? He was built like a Mack truck."

Hazel smirked at him and continued. "I wonder what he was guarding, so far the only thing worthy of a guard is us. Maybe he was guarding a main control room or an exit. If we could find a way past him then maybe we have a chance of getting everyone out of here."

Rueben had wondered the same thing when he was trying to memorize the route earlier but with how uniform the building was, that would prove rather difficult.

"Hazel, I am not even sure we could get out of this room, let alone into the other one." he muttered. "Maybe if we trust someone else with this secret of ours, we could devise a plan. Three heads are much better than one."

She shook her head, "No, we must do this alone. My letter said that more than one might make it out alive. I am sure that means only two people and not the whole group. I chose you because of your expertise in escape room knowledge, even though my first choice was Victor due to his strength and training."

Rueben opened his mouth and then shut it again without saying a word. His stomach tightened and he thought he was going to puke. He wasn't her first choice, which meant he had to play his cards wisely. He attempted to wipe the shock off his face. If she did not want to add anyone to the group then they would figure something out alone. Maybe they could save everyone else later.

He watched Hazel closely trying to figure out what she was feeling in all of this. The games had already taken so much of a toll on him that he knew that years of therapy would be required if he got out of here. He had done some dark things in these trials, and they were not over yet. Maybe she was right, if we could find another way out of here then maybe they could avoid more psychological damage.

"Well if we are going to get out of here then we need a distraction." Rueben said slowly. "Something to cause a scene so that we can slip out the door and get down the hall undetected. But that means only one of us would get to leave. That way we can vouch for one another, if you cause the distraction then I can sneak out for a little bit."

Rueben was hoping she would see the logic in this plan. He wanted to be the one to get out and look for the guarded door. If it was the control room or an exit, he could use that to his advantage. He did not quite trust Hazel with the revelation of her original choice of partner. She could be leading him to his death for all he knew. These games were known to pit players against one another for survival. He thought back to the Selected that was strapped to the wheel and shivered. That guy had formed too many connections to the others and sacrificed himself in the end. Rueben was too selfish for that. He valued his life too much. Seeing your mother taken too soon and in such a manner really puts things into perspective.

Hazel still had not responded yet, and Rueben was beginning to wonder if she could see right through him. After what seemed like forever she finally responded.

"Yes, that seems like it could work." She said hesitantly. "Now what shall this huge distraction be?"

He sat in silence for a moment. Thinking of all the possible distractions they could trigger. They could rile up some tension in the room causing a fight. Desperate ideas flickered—violence, flirtation, manipulation—but he thought Hazel had more dignity than that.

He looked over as Hazel leaned back against the wall. She placed her hands down to brace herself. The tile underneath her right hand sank into the ground with a slight click. She looked at him in surprise as she fell backwards landing on the white tile. Behind her was a gap in the wall in the shape of a door with a white bricked hallway stretching in both directions.

His mouth fell open. There was a hidden doorway in their cell that led out into the hallway.

Rueben scrambled to his feet, heart pounding.

Hazel was already sitting up, eyes wide, staring into the hallway like she'd just opened a tomb.

Neither of them spoke.

The silence was thick, humming with the possibility of escape—or something worse.

Rueben stepped forward, peering into the corridor. It looked identical to the others, but somehow… wrong. Too empty. Too quiet. Like it hadn't been touched in years.

Hazel stood, brushing dust from her palms. "I didn't mean to—"

"I know," Rueben said, voice low. "But maybe this is the way out."

Hazel raised an eyebrow.

"Not for the group," he added. "For us."

With a look between the two of them, they made a silent agreement. Standing, they both took a deep breath and stepped out into the bright white halls, feeling the sting of the cold air hitting his face.

13.

Discovery

Rueben paused adjusting to the brightness of the hall. The shower lights had been dimmed, sleep in mind. Out in the hall it was as if nothing had changed from the walk back from dinner, bright lights reflecting off the white bricks.

"Which way?" he said in a harsh whisper.

Hazel looked around blinking back tears as she tried to adjust her eyes. "Let's just head in this direction to see what we can find." She motioned to the right.

They tried to tiptoe down the hall as quietly as possible. Rueben kept hearing a faint clicking sound as the bones cracked in his big toe. Hopefully no one could hear his bones snapping like a twig in a forest, but the halls seemed rather empty.

He looked around for any signs of movement.

Not one door was ajar leaving him feeling secluded in this desolate hallway.

There did not appear to be any cameras in the hall which struck Rueben as odd. Why would they not monitor the halls in case of an attempt of escape, unless they thought the maze of halls was enough of a deterrent. Or maybe the cameras were hidden out here, to give the illusion of hope.

Crack!

Rueben winced as his toe cracked again sending the sound rippling down the hall. Hazel glanced back at him with a look of amusement on her face and he couldn't help but smile. She put her finger to her mouth signaling for him to be quiet. He mouthed the word sorry as he tried to hold in the laughter he felt bubbling up in his throat.

The tile in the halls had to be disgusting. His bare feet were already turning black. When was the last time this floor was cleaned? Everything gave the appearance of being clean, even though it was not. With the flourescent buzzing above and the uniformity of the hall, it felt like a hospital or a prison in here.

They had already walked past three convergence points in the hall. Hazel was walking with an urgency and

Rueben felt the tension bearing down on him like a weight.

Crack

Hazel was peering around the corner when she whipped around giving him an icy glare. The look on her face sent chills down his spine.

"If your stupid toe gets us caught I will cut it off myself." She said. Before Rueben had a chance to react she was talking again. "There is a door around the corner that looks different from the rest. I think it might be a control room or an exit."

Rueben peeked around the corner to find a steel door at the end of the hall. It was the same one as before. It seemed to be the only hall that had an ending while the others kept weaving in and out of themselves. The door was eerie looking as it reflected the fluorescents back at them. His breath caught in his throat forcing him to feel lightheaded. This could be the way out, or a huge advantage to help win the games. There had to be something really important behind that door.

Rueben and Hazel began to inch closer to the door, as his heart began thumping in his chest. The faint sound of machines whirring came from beyond the door, the steel seeming to amplify the sound. His blood was rushing so fast that Rueben swore that he could hear it in his ears. As they approached the door his stomach did a somersault.

Off to the right of the door was a black box with a red light illuminated. Of course there would be a key card required to enter this room. He looked around. This is one giant escape room. There had to be another way behind that door. There was no sign of any guards, so no access to a key card. The halls were clear of any kind of equipment to try and dismantle the card reader. He sighed and rolled his neck trying to relieve some of the tension and that is when he saw it. His eyes narrowed as he contemplated the logistics of the idea that was forming in his head. With a slow nod to himself he turned back to Hazel.

"Hazel!" he whispered getting her attention. She was messing with the box trying to take it off. "Come here, I have a plan."

She walked over to him without a sound.

"You see that speaker right there?" he said pointing to the speaker that was embedded in the ceiling tile. It looked just like all the others scattered throughout the building. "I am going to hoist you up there and I need you to get it down for me."

"Can you hold me up that high?" she said taking in his weak looking stature.

"I am pretty sure if I squat down low enough I can get you on my shoulders and you can reach it. The ceiling is not that high." He said trying to ignore her comment.

Rueben steadied Hazel on his shoulders as she reached for the speaker embedded in the ceiling tile.

"Careful," he whispered. "If it's wired into the same control panel as the door, we might be able to short the reader."

Hazel pried the speaker casing loose, revealing a tangle of red, black, and green wires. Rueben swayed a little but quickly regained his balance. They had to move fast for this to work.

"Which one?" she asked.

"Red's usually power. If we cross it with the green—"

A spark popped and a loud shriek emmited from the speaker. The lights in the hall dimmed slightly and Rueben wondered if they might go out completely. The red light on the card reader flickered, then went dark.

Rueben's heart pounded. "That's our window. Let's move."

He bent down and Hazel hit the ground running as she reached for the door. By the time Rueben had gotten back to his feet she was standing in the open doorway motioning for him to hurry.

They let the door softly click behind them and took in the room with bated breath. The room was only lit by the computer screens that completely covered the entire wall in front of them, with monitors beeping around the room. There seemed to be cameras everywhere and Rueben was trying to see the exact placement of all of them, but the screens were flashing too quickly, moving on to the next section.

He glanced at Hazel and noticed a look of shock and terror on her face. He looked back to see what she was looking at and saw it. In the center of the screens was one that was frozen. It was very pixelated, and the time stamp was from the previous night. He squinted trying to see better.

He looked back to Hazel and she held a finger up to her mouth, cocking her head to the side. Listening. Maybe it wasn't the screen that had caught her attention, he thought to himself.

That is when he heard it, the soft thud of boots hitting the ground.

He glanced back up at the screens and saw two Masked guards sprinting down the hall. The thudding was getting louder.

"Shit" Hazel said under her breath.

They were really close now and Rueben didn't know what to do.

Hazel grabbed his wrist and yanked him behind the door. They were pressed up against one another and Rueben was thankful for the darkness of the room, as his cheeks began to heat up.

The door swung open and Rueben caught his breath as two big brutes barreled through the door. He waited… one…two….Fuck it.

Without hashing out his plan, Rueben rushed forward barreling into the closest guard. He tipped forward falling into the other man and then they both hit the ground in a tangled mess as they flipped over an office chair.

"Let's Go!" Hazel yelled from the doorway.

Rueben turned and ran for the open door.

As he crossed the threshold heading back into the hall, he turned just in time to see one of the Masked getting up. He yanked the door from Hazel's grasp and slammed it shut just as the guard lunged.

He heard the beep of the key card and the door began to open toward them.

"Help me" he screamed at Hazel, and they both put all their body weight into the door, sealing it shut once more.

Rueben balled up his fist and smashed it into the card reader. The black plastic shattered into pieces and sliced his wrist as the shrapnel went flying. He quickly covered his wrist to stop the flow from dripping on the floor.

Blood pulsed beneath his fingers as he pressed the wound. The latch clicked. Rueben smirked—half pain, half victory. Hazel said nothing.

14.

Punishment

Rueben laid there staring at the ceiling. The lights were beginning to flicker back on, signaling that morning had arrived. The lights hummed to life, slicing through the eerie silence. He thought back to the events of last night and gave his wrist a slight rub, a twinge of pain shooting up his arm.

A corner of the bed sheet was wrapped around his wrist sticky and wet from the blood still trying to ooze from his open wound. He glanced down at his arm ensuring that it was still covered by the sleeve of his jacket.

Movement was happening around the room as everyone started their morning routines. Ivy headed to the showers to get clean before breakfast, Natalie was washing her face in the sink, and Victor was lacing up his boots. He glanced over to where Hazel was sitting and saw that she was staring at him from the edge of her bed. The blanket was wrapped around her body like a protective layer of fabric.

When they had returned to the room last night, Rueben had slipped into one of the showers to clean himself off and Hazel had snuck back into bed without even acknowledging what had happened. Rueben wondered where her thoughts were going but was too nervous to ask. What if she wasn't prepared to help him anymore because of how reckless he was? He pulled at his sleeve to cover the pinkish brown sheet that had started to peek out from underneath his jacket. The group did not need to know what happened last night. His life might well depend on it.

The lights buzzed overhead, brighter now, but still no sign of breakfast. Rueben sat up slowly, his stomach twisting—not from hunger, but from dread.

Natalie glanced at the clock on the wall. "They're late," she said, voice low.

Victor grunted, tugging his boot tighter. "They're never late."

Hazel hadn't moved. She was still wrapped in her blanket, eyes now fixed on the door.

Rueben opened his mouth to speak, to ask if anyone else felt it too—that something was wrong—but the words stuck. His wrist throbbed beneath the jacket. He didn't deserve to ask questions.

Then the intercom crackled.

"TRIAL THREE BEGINS NOW. ALL PARTICIPANTS, REPORT TO THE STAGING CORRIDOR. NO BREAKFAST WILL BE SERVED."

The room fell silent.

Rueben felt every eye shift toward him. Not directly. Not accusing. But searching.

Hazel stood first. She didn't look at him, just made a beeline to the door, face stoic, movements rigid.

Rueben got up to follow her, wincing as he used his hurt wrist for leverage.

The tension pressed against Rueben's ribs like a vice. No one spoke, but the silence was thick with dread. They were being led to a new trial and there would not even be any breakfast. He should have eaten more food at the feast last night.

"If I ever meet the lunatic behind these rules, I'll strangle them with my bare hands—and I'll laugh while the light drains from their eyes." Victor cracked his neck and shoved past Rueben to the front of the group.

"Honestly, I might help you with that" Trinity says with a pull on her lips, a slight smile showing through.

"I second that notion" said Ivy with a sadistic grin coating her face.

Maybe hunger and desperation could do what fear never did—bind them together. They could all work together to get out of here, but first Rueben needed to run it past Hazel. He already felt like he was on thin ice with her, and she was an integral part of this escape plan. He inched closer to her trying to get her attention, but her eyes were glued to the guard in front of her.

The hallway opened up to a large corridor with double doors standing alone at the end of the hall. They had not come this way at all on the way to dinner and he did not recall seeing these doors on his excursion from the night before. This place really was a huge maze.

The Masked guard at the head of the group pushed both the doors open and a cold blast of moist air hit them all in the face. It was a large room with cement walls to the left and right and a gaping hole directly in front of them. Green algae slithered down the damp walls, slick and glistening like rot come alive. Mold and copper stinging his nostrils, making his face scrunch in disgust. On either side of the room was a yellow slide, dark with stains, that led into the dark chasm below. Rueben could hear the faint dripping of water. Metal railings rusted and brown, the only thing stopping them from falling off the edge of the platform in front of them. The two slides intertwined and twisted as they led into the darkness below.

There was a slight gurgle and then the crackle of a speaker coming to life. It sounded as if it had been submerged in water, forcing Rueben to wonder why everything in the room was wet.

"WELCOME TO TRIAL NUMBER THREE. BEFORE YOU LIES TWO SLIDES. TWO SIDES TO EVEN OUT THE BALANCE. LIFE AND DEATH. ONE SLIDE BRINGS YOU TO THE NEXT TRIAL AND ONE LEADS YOU TO CERTAIN DEATH. CHOOSE WISELY. WILL TRINITY AND HAZEL PLEASE STEP FORWARD."

Just as the room fell silent, several Masked guards entered the room holding black pieces of cloth. In unison, almost as if they were mechanical. They gathered everyone in a circle and blind folded each player.

"Good luck," one of them growled.

"They aren't going to let you guys see which slide we choose," said Hazel from somewhere off to the right of the group.

Rueben felt his stomach drop like a stone sinking in water, ripples of unease swimming through his gut. Why did she sound so calm? Was she hiding something, or was she detaching herself in an attempt to sound tough. A form of misdirection for anyone watching what was unfolding.

With his sight stripped away, Rueben's other senses surged—every breath, every shuffle, every whisper magnified. The sound of labored breathing echoed through his head as he tried to listen for cues. What was happening?

"Well, are we going to pick the same slide or each take one?" Trinity asked, voice shaky.

"You heard them, one leads to death and the other leads to the next trial. We need to pick opposite slides, no sense in both of us dying. One of us will have to live to try and signal the others which way is safe," said Hazel

"How will you guys choose?" asked Rueben. "What if you wanted the same slide?"

"You will have to come to a mutual decision," said Natalie.

Rueben felt a presence behind his right shoulder and he tensed.

"IF I die, you need to still try to get out of here. You know where the control room is, that is your way out," Hazel whispered in his ear. So close that the others wouldn't have been able to hear her. "How do you want to do this?" she said louder, making Rueben jump.

"Let's go to the edge to see if we can see anything," said Trinity. "Maybe, our eyes will adjust and we can see which slide leads to danger."

Rueben could hear the splash of boots as they echoed off the walls. The puddles in the room becoming more evident with each step they took.

"It's no use," said Hazel. "It is so dark down there, and it seems to go on forever."

"Just make the decision for us," said Trinity. "I don't have any family outside of here. No one will be waiting for me anyway."

The crack in her voice sent chills down Ruebens spine. The sound of defeat lingering in the air. Trinity choked back a sob as she walked across the room. The crinkle of a jacket told Rueben that the two girls were hugging.

"Are you sure this is what you want?" asked Hazel sniffling. The sound cut through the dark like a blade. Rueben flinched. The sound was too familiar—too much like the way his mother had cried the night before she died as she begged him to stay home. His breath caught. The room vanished. He was back in that hallway, the cold brass doorknob grasped in his hand, the silence before the sirens.

Flashbacks riddled through his mind. A cold sweat breaking out over his skin, like a glass of ice water melting in the heat. He shivered, rubbing his arms together trying to warm up. A sharp pain pulsed up his arm into his shoulder, snapping him out of the memory—and the guilt that never stopped gnawing at him for leaving her alone that night.

Rueben blinked hard, lashes rubbing against the blindfold. He was trying to force the memory back into its cage. The air in the room felt thinner now, like it was being siphoned away. Hazel and Trinity had stopped speaking. The silence pressed in.

Then came the sound—boots scraping against metal, a jacket rustling, breath hitching.

Hazel's voice broke through. "I'll take the right."

Trinity didn't argue. "Then I'll take the left."

Rueben's pulse thudded in his ears. He couldn't see them clearly, but he could feel the tension radiating off their bodies. The slides stretched ahead—identical in shape, texture, and angle. No distinct markings. No clues. No mercy.

"You sure?" Hazel asked, voice cracking.

"I'm sure," Trinity whispered.

A beat passed. Then movement. A body shifting. A breath held.

Then— a distant splash followed by a soft squelching sound.

Rueben flinched but didn't speak. He didn't know who had gone first. Didn't know who had survived.

Natalie stepped forward, her voice low but firm. "That was Trial Three."

The blindfold was ripped from his face by a strong, calloused hand. He blinked against the sudden light, eyes struggling to adjust. Both slides stood desolate and empty, no hints as to which one was the way out.

The Masked were standing in the corners of the room, staring blankly off into the distance. No emotions could be seen underneath the devil faces they wore. One of them stepped forward pulling a small remote control from his jacket pocket. The remote had two buttons on the face, one red and one green.

He held the remote up in the air for all of us to see. Hitting the red button, the room was plunged into darkness, the only light coming from the remote control. The green light disappeared as the Masked pushed down on the button. A loud groan echoed off the cement, the noise grinding into Rueben's head like a drill.

A sharp jolt threw Rueben to the ground as the floor beneath them began to spin.

"I think I am going to be sick." Ivy groaned behind him, or was it in front of him?

The room spun for what seemed like hours, but Rueben knew it must have only been a minute or two. Loud thuds reverberated off the walls and finally they ground to a stop. The lights flickered back on with a sickening hum.

The room now had four walls instead of the three, the dark chasm seemingly gone. The room was now smaller, but the slides still remained. He turned slowly, dread thickening with every glance. He realized that the Masked had now dissapeared and they were all left alone in the room, with nothing but the slides as ways out.

"Trial three is not over," he said softly.

15.

The Decision

Rueben felt like the walls were closing in, and maybe they were. Disoriented and confused he turned to the closest slide, which was to the left. Or was it the right?

The room tilted again, or maybe it was just his stomach. The slides blurred into one another—identical, indifferent, like twin mouths waiting to swallow them whole.

"Well which slide do we take? That seems to be the only way out of this hell hole," Ivy said as she made her way over to where he was standing.

"Uh….. Guys!" Hazel's voice came drifting up the slide, but it sounded like it was echoing around the room. Did it come from the other slide? "Trinity didn't make it."

Rueben's breath caught. The name ricocheted off the walls like a curse, each repetition more hollow than the last. Trinity didn't make it. Trinity didn't make it.

The words seemed to keep repeating. Repeating. Repeating. Repeating.

Gripping the sides of the slide in an attempt to regain control, Rueben looked over at Ivy. Her mouth was open, she was searching for the right words, but nothing came out. Accepting defeat she closed her mouth and just looked at Rueben a single tear in her eye. It wasn't grief yet. It was something rawer—shock, maybe, or the slow realization that survival didn't mean safety. He grabbed her hand in his and gave it a light squeeze, a silent confirmation that the group needed one another.

"I took the slide on the right, so take that one and get down here," her voice was sliding back and forth across the cement walls, seemingly coming from everywhere and nowhere.

"The room took us for a spin. Can you climb back into the slide so that we can hear which one you are coming from, everything is echoing up here," Rueben called out in a brief spell of clarity.

"No such luck guys, they are too far up for me to reach. Let me see if I can find something to help."

Rueben sighed deeply feeling defeated. If they could not find a way to figure out the correct slide, then more than one person would die in this trial.

"Well make a decision soon, or I am going to start throwing people down slides," said Victor.

Rueben tensed, Victor's presence felt like static—loud, unpredictable, dangerous. Rueben didn't trust him, but he didn't trust the silence either.

"We could all just throw you down instead," retorted Ivy. "Maybe use your body as a shield for whatever awaits us at the bottom."

Rueben tried to hide his smirk as he stood to face Victor. "What we need to do is work together for once. There is nothing in the *rules* that says that this is a free for all. We can try and make it out of here together."

The words fell out of his mouth before he could stop himself. The last thing he wanted was to work with Victor Kane. He would rather take his chances on the slide, but seeing Ivy show some vulnerability a few moments ago was the humanity reminder he needed. They were all just trying to survive and he could not put blame on anyone for putting themselves first.

Rueben looked between both slides—smooth, curved fiberglass, dulled yellow under the harsh overhead lights. They looked like playground equipment warped by what appeared to be years of use. Identical. Deceptive. Purposeful.

"Ivy," he said quietly, "if we choose wrong…"

"I know." Her voice was low, steady. The tear had dried, but something desolate settled in her eyes. "We lose someone else."

A low vibration hummed through the floor, subtle but unmistakable. Ivy shifted her weight, instinctively bracing herself.

"What was that?" she asked, her voice barely above a whisper.

Rueben didn't answer. He was listening—straining—for Hazel's voice.

Then, faintly: *"Found something. Might help. Hold on."*

The sound was warped, stretched like it had been pulled through water. Rueben clenched his jaw. The room was playing tricks on them.

Ivy moved toward the slide on the right, crouching beside it. "No light," she murmured. "But I think I hear something. A scraping sound?"

Rueben tilted his head, holding his breath- blood pounding in his ears from the strain. Shifting his weight he tried to get as close to the edge of the slide as possible without falling down.

There! He heard it too. The sound so faint, he almost missed it.

Tink. Tink. Tink.

"Are you throwing something in the slide?" he yelled down as he stuck his whole head down the slide. Ivy's hands grabbed his waist to hold him steady.

"Yeah! I found some marble or something chipped off one of the columns down here," her voice came bounding up the slide. Louder this time, almost as if she was closer.

"Great, we are coming down." He turned back to the group. "I'll go first, then Ivy, Natalie, and then you," he said pointing at Victor.

"Who died and made you boss?" he asked as he bucked up to Rueben.

"Poor choice of words douchebag," said Natalie piping up. "Trinity is dead, and we could very well be next if we aren't careful. So shut up and do as he says."

Rueben was shocked. Natalie was so much smaller than Victor and had sided with him before. What could have brought on this change?

Victor's jaw twitched. "You think you know what's best now?" His voice was low, almost amused.

Natalie didn't flinch. "I think Rueben does. And I think you're scared of that."

A beat passed. Victor's eyes flicked to Rueben, then to the slide.

"Scared?" he echoed. "You think I'm scared of that puny little punk?"

Rueben opened his mouth to defend himself—he was small, sure, but puny wasn't the word he'd use. Not anymore. He closed it again, the words curdling behind his teeth. Victor had threatened him more than once, and Rueben had learned that survival sometimes meant silence.

"No," Natalie said. "You're scared of not being in control," her voice was steady, calculating. She was reading him like a book.

Victor scoffed in an attempt to shrug off her comment. But the shift in his eyes confirmed her statement. Rueben couldn't blame the guy. They were all being controlled by the Masked. This was their game, and they were the pawns—scrambling for scraps of power in a rigged arena.

Rueben stepped toward the slide, but Ivy caught his arm.

"You sure you want to go first?" she asked, voice low.

He glanced at her. Her expression was unreadable— not fear, exactly, but something close. A guarded curiosity.

"I'm already halfway there," Rueben said. "Someone has to go."

Ivy's gaze flicked to the dark mouth of the slide. "You think it's safe?"

Rueben hesitated. "No. But waiting up here isn't, either."

Ivy nodded slowly. "Fair point. This whole place is a coin toss."

Rueben almost smiled. Ivy had a way of making dread sound poetic.

He looked back at the others. Victor was still brooding, Natalie standing firm. The room felt like it was holding its breath.

Rueben turned to Ivy. "If I scream, don't follow."

Ivy raised an eyebrow. "If you scream, I'm definitely following.

With one final breath he climbed into the slide, looking down toward the first curve that led into the darkness below. He was taking a huge risk by going first. Death could be waiting for him at the bottom, mocking him. How ironic that the thing that would take him out would be a symbol of joy and hope in the real world? If he made it out of here, he would never look at a playground the same way again.

He pushed off and started his descent. Despite how awful the slide looked from the room above, it was surprisingly slick. He was picking up a lot of speed and he felt like he was losing control. He was trying to grip the sides in an attempt to slow himself down, but the slide was too wide. Down, down he went, twisting and turning so much he thought he was going to be sick. Then he saw the light. Was he dead or was this just the end of the slide?

Before he could react a rush of air met his face and brought tears to his eyes. He braced for the impact and felt cold water splashing up to hit him. His breath seized just as his body hit concrete, hard. The air burst from his lungs in a single, choking gasp. He clawed for the surface—only to realize the water was barely two feet deep. All he had to do was sit up.

Grunting, Rueben pushed himself upright and turned to look at the slide. It hung about five feet off the ground.

Definitely reachable.

Hazel could have climbed back up—if she'd really tried.

Rueben wiped water from his eyes and stepped a little closer to the slide.

"I'm alive!" he shouted, voice echoing off damp concrete. "It's shallow—just brace for impact!"

He waited, chest still heaving, as the silence stretched. Then came the sound of movement above—metal creaking, a body shifting.

Victor landed next, arms flailing, cursing as he hit the water and scrambled upright.

"Hell of a ride," he muttered, shaking out his sleeves.

Natalie followed, more controlled but still gasping as she surfaced. Ivy came last, landing with a grunt and immediately scanning the room.

"I told you to be come down behind me…" he muttered.

Rueben helped her up, then turned to take in their surroundings.

The space was massive—easily the size of a gymnasium, maybe larger. Thick marble columns rose from the shallow pool, stretching up into the shadows. The ceiling was lost in darkness, but a few flickering bulbs cast sickly light across the water. The air smelled of mildew, rust, and something faintly metallic—blood, maybe.

A narrow walkway led deeper into the room, flanked by jagged metal railings. At the far end, something glinted.

Rueben squinted. "Is that—?"

Natalie screamed.

Everyone spun toward her. She was frozen, one hand clamped over her mouth, the other pointing.

There, impaled on a cluster of rusted spikes between two columns, was Trinity.

Her body was twisted unnaturally, limbs askew, eyes wide open.

Rueben felt the breath leave his lungs again—this time not from impact, but from shock.

Rueben took a step toward Trinity's body, but stopped short. The spikes were jagged, rusted, and slick with blood. Her limbs hung limp, her head tilted at an unnatural angle. No one spoke.

Then a voice broke the silence.

"I think I found a way out."

Hazel stepped from behind one of the columns, soaked and pale, her eyes wide but strangely calm.

Victor turned sharply. "Where the hell have you been?"

Hazel ignored him. "There's a tunnel behind the far column. I didn't go far, but it looks like—"

A low gurgling sound cut her off.

It came from the slide.

Rueben turned just in time to see water surging from the mouth—not trickling, but rushing, like a broken dam. The pool around them rippled, then churned violently.

"Move!" Ivy shouted, grabbing Natalie's arm.

The water hit Trinity's body first.

It slammed into the spikes with brutal force, tearing flesh from bone. Her torso twisted, then split, one arm ripped free and flung across the room like a discarded doll. The sound was wet and final.

Natalie screamed again, backing away as blood spread through the water like ink.

Rueben stumbled, nearly falling as the current surged around his legs. The water was rising fast.

Hazel's voice was barely audible over the chaos. "Trial Four," she said. "It's starting."

Rueben surged forward with the water, drowning in trepidation.

16.

Rising Tide

The water was rising fast, swallowing the floor in thick, red swells. Rueben didn't look back at what was left of Trinity. He couldn't. Hazel was already halfway to the tunnel, her silhouette framed by the flickering lights. Ivy clutched Natalie's wrist, frozen between grief and motion.

"Move," Rueben said, voice hoarse. "Now."

He started to move forward through the water that was rising around his legs and waist. The girls began to move, the fear of drowning overcoming them. He glanced back to make sure they were all staying close together and saw Ivy slip underneath the surface. He reached out fast, grabbing her wrist just as she slid past. He yanked hard, pulling her back into the chaos. The water was moving quickly like the rapids in a river—unrelenting, unforgiving.

"We gotta move quick if we want to stay alive," Rueben shouted. It felt like the water was so loud now, rushing past them all, hurtling debris around in swirls of blood red foam.

Natalie screamed and Rueben turned just in time to see Trinity's severed arm float by.

The amount of therapy that all of them would need if they made it out of here would keep therapists in business for years to come.

They were closing in on the tunnel. Hazel already disappearing into the dim corridor.

The tunnel swallowed them whole. Rueben barely registered the moment the current shifted—one second, he was dragging Ivy forward, the next they were all tumbling into the narrow passage, water sloshing around their knees. The walls pressed in, slick with condensation, humming faintly like they were alive.

Ivy gasped behind him. "I can't—Rueben, I can't breathe."

"You're breathing," he said, not turning. "Just keep moving."

Hazel didn't speak. She moved like she knew the way, like the tunnel was hers.

Then they rounded the bend.

The passage ended in a blank wall. No door. No markings. Just concrete.

Natalie whimpered. Ivy stopped breathing again.

Hazel cursed into the void.

Rueben stepped forward and pressed his palm to the wall. It was warm.

Victor had said nothing the entire time. Not when Natalie screamed, not when Ivy had nearly drowned and Rueben had pulled her up, not when Hazel cursed the room like it could hear her.

But when they hit the wall—when Rueben pressed his hand against the blank concrete and whispered, "No, no, no…"—Victor snapped.

He slammed both fists into the wall, over and over, the sound echoing like gunshots. His breath came in ragged bursts. "You think this is it?" he shouted. "You think this is how we die? In a fucking hallway?"

Ivy backed away. Natalie sobbed harder. Hazel didn't move.

Rueben stared at Victor, stunned who was now bleeding from his knuckles and screaming at the walls.

The tunnel groaned—a deep, guttural sound like the earth itself was choking. Dust poured from the ceiling in thick sheets. Ivy screamed. Natalie ducked. Rueben turned just in time to see a slab of concrete shear loose from the wall.

It hit him hard. His arm—the one that was already injured—jerked back, and pain lanced through the old wound. The wrap tore. Blood bloomed fresh and fast, soaking through the fabric before it was ripped away by the rush of falling debris.

He staggered.

Hazel was there.

Her hand gripped his wrist but not the injured one. Her eyes—usually so calculating—flashed wide with something Rueben couldn't name. Fear? Concern?

"You're bleeding," she said, voice low, urgent.

"I'm fine," he lied.

She didn't let go. Her fingers tightened. "No, you're not."

Then the tunnel gave another shudder, and she pulled him forward, shielding him with her body for a split second before the dust swallowed them both.

The dust was suffocating. Rueben couldn't see, couldn't breathe. His lungs burned with every gasp, and the ground beneath him felt slick—muddy, unstable. Somewhere behind him, the tunnel groaned again, and water surged in a sudden wave, cold and fast.

Hazel's grip didn't loosen.

She pulled him forward, half dragging, half swimming through the rising sludge. Her voice was hoarse, barely audible over the roar of collapsing stone.

"Keep moving!"

Rueben stumbled, his injured arm useless, blood mixing with the water in dark ribbons. He slipped once, went under, came up choking. Hazel was already ahead, clawing at the edge of a broken wall, her fingers raw and bleeding.

He reached her just as another wave hit, slamming them both against the jagged tunnel mouth.

Hazel shoved him upward.

"Go!"

He didn't argue. He scrambled, slipped, felt her push again, and then he was out—coughing, gasping, blinking against the light of the main room.

Hazel followed seconds later, soaked and shaking.

The others were already on their feet, wide-eyed and panicked. Ivy was crying. Natalie was shouting something Rueben couldn't hear. Victor was slumped against the far wall, dazed.

Rueben turned to Hazel. She looked at him—really looked—and for a moment, he saw the same fear in her that he felt in himself.

Then the ceiling cracked again.

"We need to move," Hazel said, voice steady now. "There's another way out. There has to be."

The main room was chaos. Dust hung in the air like smoke. The water was still rising. They were on the far side of the massive room now, opposite the slides and gushing water. The water was at their knees again but rising fast. Ivy was curled up on a pillar, knees to her chest, rocking slightly. Her breaths came in short, sharp bursts—too fast, too shallow.

Rueben knelt beside her, ignoring the pain in his arm.

"Ivy," he said gently. "You're okay. We're out. You're safe."

She didn't respond.

He reached out, touched her shoulder. "Look at me."

Her eyes met his—wild, unfocused.

"I almost drowned," she whispered. "When I was six. Fell into a pool. No one saw. I couldn't scream. I just... sank."

Rueben didn't speak. He let her words settle, let her breathe.

"I thought I was going to die in that tunnel," she said. "I thought it was happening again."

"You didn't," Rueben said. "You're here. You made it."

She nodded slowly, tears streaking through the dust on her face.

Then she looked past him, toward the far wall. Her brow furrowed.

"There," she said, voice steadier. "That grate—it's loose. The water's flowing toward it."

Rueben turned to look and saw it near the center of the room. The water was filling up the room fast, but the grate was draining, slowly. The grate was half-submerged, rusted, and bent at one corner. It looked barely big enough to crawl through.

Hazel stepped forward, eyes narrowing. "You think it leads out?"

"I don't know," Ivy said. "But it's moving. It's not sealed."

Hazel turned to Rueben. "If it's a way out, we take it."

Rueben looked at Ivy. She was still trembling, but her eyes were clear now. Determined.

"You found it," he said. "You saved us."

"We'll have to hold our breaths and let the current take us," Victor said flatly. "It either leads out... or we die, and humanity dies with us."

Rueben had forgotten that their lives were tied to the fates of all humanity until that very moment. He felt nervous and scared, but looking around the room there weren't many options.

"We either die when this room finally fills up, or we die trying to escape. Either way humanity is doomed. At least if we go into the grate we are giving them a fighting chance," Rueben glanced at the others for confirmation.

Hazel silently nodded.

Ivy gave him a weak smile.

Victor sighed. "Then I guess that is our way out."

17.

The Undertow

Hazel moved first, making a beeline for the grate. The rest of the group followed close behind, their steps quick and uncertain.

The water was rising fast—this might be their only chance.

It swirled around their legs, circling the grate like a bathtub drain. Rueben had always wondered where the water went after a shower. He was about to find out.

Hazel reached the grate first but didn't go in. She crouched beside it, water lapping at her chest now, her fingers scrabbling at the metal. It wouldn't budge.

Ivy stopped just behind her, panting, soaked to the shoulders. The others clustered close, eyes wide, breaths shallow.

The water was rising fast—too fast. It churned around them, dark and hungry, circling the grate like it had somewhere to be. Rueben felt it pulling at him, dragging him toward the unknown.

"We don't know what's down there," Ivy said, voice trembling.

"We know what's up here," Rueben said. "And I'm done playing their game."

Hazel gritted her teeth, bracing herself against the current, trying again. The grate groaned but held. Rueben moved to help, but his injured arm gave out, pain lancing through his shoulder.

Victor stepped in without a word. He planted his feet, gripped the edge, and heaved.

The grate gave way with a shriek of metal.

Hazel didn't look back. She nodded once—and dropped.

The decision came like a snap.

One by one, they followed. No second guesses. No regrets.

And then everything slowed.

Rueben plunged into the current. It seized him instantly, twisting, dragging, ripping the air from his lungs like it had a right to it. Light vanished. Sound warped. His body felt too slow, too soft, like it didn't belong to him anymore.

He reached for the others but saw nothing—just the grate above, shrinking, fading, gone.

The masked man could keep his cameras.

They were going to survive.

Even if it meant drowning first.

Rueben plunged deeper into the current.

It hit him like a fist—cold, crushing, alive. His shoulder slammed into the tunnel wall, a jagged edge tearing through fabric and skin. Pain shot up his arm, white-hot and blinding. He tried to scream, but the water ripped the sound from his throat.

Then the memories came.

Not gently. Not like dreams.

Like knives.

Silas was in front of him. Trial One. Rueben had held the vial in his hand, fingers trembling. He'd looked between Silas and the vial, —and Silas who had smiled, calm, trusting. Rueben hadn't spoken. Hadn't moved. Just watched as Silas lifted the glass and drank.

His lips turned blue before the glass shattered on the floor, broken into a million pieces… Just like Rueben.

He had tried to convince himself it was strategy. That he hadn't known.

But he had.

The current twisted him, dragging him deeper. His body spun, limbs flailing, lungs burning.

Then his mother.

Not the real one—the nightmare version. The one who stood in the bedroom, holding a glass of something dark. Rueben had tried to warn her, but failed. She'd smiled, the way she used to when he was little and scared of thunderstorms.

"It's okay, baby," she'd said. "It's just a game."

She drank.

Her body hit the floor with a sound he couldn't forget.

No, that wasn't how any of this had happened.

Rueben clawed at the water, kicked against the pull, but it was like swimming through cement. His lungs screamed. His thoughts blurred. He couldn't tell if he was sinking or rising.

They weren't going to make it.

This wasn't escape. This was suicide.

But then—Hazel's voice, distant and muted: "Rueben, move!" He could barely hear her under the water.

He was drifting, losing the fight.

Suddenly strong hands wrapped around him.

Dragging.

A swell in his chest, rib cracking.

Spitting.

His eyes opened, lungs burning, gasping for air.

18.

The Underbelly

Rueben opened his eyes to see Victor standing over him.

"You saved me?" Rueben asked as he choked on water.

Victor was the last person he expected to be saving him.

"Trust me, I thought about leaving you there, but you are actually useful," Victor said. For a split second, Rueben thought he saw something real flicker in Victor's eyes—regret, maybe. But it vanished too fast to name.

Rueben sat up on his elbows and looked around. The room was dark and smelt of mold. The walls were reinforced cement and Rueben could see the water still rushing out of the pipe that he had dropped from. Water pooled beneath the pipe before rushing into a separate drainage system. Pipes crisscrossed the ceiling, twisting like veins. One massive pipe stretched down a hallway to the left, its hum louder than the rest.

"We fell into a drainage system" Rueben said.

"Congrats Sherlock, now tell me something I don't know," Victor retorted.

"Do you have to be an ass all the time," came a voice from behind them.

Rueben turned to see Ivy emerging from the darkness followed by Hazel and Natalie.

Ivy was slightly limping, but her attitude was back so that was a good sign. Hazel had a cut on her forehead that was slowly oozing blood and Natalie had a gash on her knee.

"What is this place?" Rueben asked

"I am not sure, but I don't think it was part of the trial." said Hazel.

"Maybe we can find a way out of here," Natalie offered, her eyes lighting up.

"I say we follow this large pipe, it might lead us out of here," Rueben pointed above their heads to the pipe that led down the hall.

"Worth a shot," said Victor as he shoved past Rueben who was still sitting on the ground.

Ivy offered him a hand and he took it, using her to test his weight to see if anything was broken.

Rueben followed Hazel and Natalie down the corridor, the soles of his shoes echoing against the concrete walls, each step amplifying his uncertainty. Ivy was at his side and gave him a wry smile. He tried to smile back but he couldn't find the energy. The hallway was narrow, windowless, and lit by rows of edison bulbs in metal casings, like they had just stepped into an old mine shaft. Their yellow hue made the hall feel like a tunnel that was moments from collapse, the soft hum making him uneasy. The air smelled faintly of antiseptic and something older—like mildew and forgotten paper.

Hazel didn't speak. Her shoulders were squared; her pace deliberate. Rueben tried to match it, but his legs felt like they were moving through syrup. Every step forward felt like a betrayal of instinct.

They passed closed doors, each marked only by a number. No labels. No clues. Just sterile anonymity.

Room 17.

Room 18.

Room 19.

They stopped.

The door in front of them was slightly ajar. No number. Just a sliver of darkness between the frame and the threshold.

Rueben's breath caught. Something about the door felt wrong—not dangerous, exactly, but off. Like it had been left open on purpose. Like it was waiting.

Hazel pushed it open.

The room beyond was colder. Vastly colder. The lighting shifted from industrial to somber—three dim bulbs hung from the ceiling like pendulums, casting long shadows across the floor. Over each of the five desks, a reading lamp glowed with a sickly yellow hue, spotlighting scattered papers and unplugged headsets.

Five monitors. All dark.

The walls were lined with metal shelves, each stacked with identical white boxes. No markings. No dust. No signs of recent use—but everything felt curated, preserved. Like someone had left in a hurry but planned to return.

Rueben stepped inside, slower than Hazel. The silence was thicker here, like the room itself was holding its breath.

"I'll keep watch," Victor said from out in the hall.

Hazel moved to the nearest desk and picked up a manila folder. Her fingers hesitated at the edge, as if she expected it to bite.

Hazel flipped open the folder. Her eyes scanned the page, then froze.

"Subject 47," she read aloud. "No kin. Deceased."

She didn't say anything else, but the words hung in the air like a toxin.

Natalie stepped closer. "Deceased? As in… they died during a trial?"

Hazel nodded slowly. "Or before it. There's no date. Just a stamp."

Victor leaned against the doorframe, arms crossed. "Guess they don't waste ink on the details."

Rueben moved to the next desk, his fingers trailing across the surface like he was afraid it might burst into flames. He opened a folder. Another subject. Another stamp.

"Subject 12. Deceased."

Natalie opened a drawer and pulled out a stack of wristbands. Each one had a number. No names.

"These weren't contestants," she whispered. "They were test runs."

Ivy crouched beside a shelf and tugged out a box. Inside: a blood-stained shirt, folded like laundry. She didn't speak. Just stared.

Rueben opened another folder. Then another. All the same. Numbers. No kin. Deceased.

Then he saw it.

A folder half-buried beneath a stack of papers. His fingers trembled as he pulled it free.

Rueben Bentley.

No number. No stamp.

Just his name.

He opened it slowly. The first page was blank. The second held a photo—his photo. Taken from above, like a security cam. His eyes were closed. He looked sedated.

Natalie stepped behind him. "Is that—?"

Rueben didn't answer. His jaw clenched. He flipped to the next page.

Vitals. Bloodwork. Psychological profile. Notes in red ink.

"Subject shows high resilience. Unpredictable under stress. Recommend isolation."

Hazel's voice was barely a whisper. "They were watching you."

Rueben flipped to the next page. "They still are." Photos lined the page. Him at home. At work. At the grocery store. Casual. Unaware. Hunted. There were even photos of him in the trials.

He flipped the page again—but before he could read the contents, a hand slammed down on the desk beside him.

Victor's voice cut through the silence. "We've got company."

Then came the sound.

A door slammed open. They were close. Too close.

Three Masked figures burst into the room, fast and aggressive. One lunged for Hazel, another for Rueben, the third went for Ivy.

Victor didn't hesitate—he tackled the nearest one, driving him into a desk with a crash. Punching him repeatedly in the face. Hazel ducked low, grabbing a lamp and swinging it upward into his jaw. Glass shattering upon impact. Rueben shoved the second Masked before he had a chance to recover forcing him to the ground.

Ivy kicked him in the gut in an effort to keep him on the ground.

"Run!" she shouted to the others.

Natalie grabbed a chair and hurled it at the guard who was attempting to get back up, knocking him into the shelves. Boxes tumbled. Papers scattered. Then the shelf tipped over on top of him, pinning him to the ground. Finally.

The group surged into the hallway, breath ragged, feet pounding against concrete. The corridor stretched straight ahead—no turns, no cover.

They ran.

Victor led the way, Hazel close behind. Rueben pulled Ivy forward, Natalie at their heels. Behind them, the Masked were down—groaning, unmoving.

For a moment, Rueben thought they might make it.

Then the hallway ahead darkened.

More Masked emerged from the shadows. Not three. Not five.

Dozens.

Black uniforms. Blank oni type masks. Silent.

Victor skidded to a stop. "Back!"

They turned, sprinting the other way—but the corridor behind them was no longer empty.

Another wave of Masked was advancing. Coordinated. Calm. A wall of faceless control.

Hazel slowed. "We're boxed in."

Rueben looked around. No exits. No vents. No weapons left.

Victor raised his fists again, blood streaked across his knuckles. "We're not going back."

Then one Masked stepped forward. His mask bore large horns and huge sharpened teeth. His voice was calm. Cold.

"You are."

Rueben's chest heaved. Ivy gripped his arm. Natalie's eyes darted, searching for something—anything.

There was nothing.

Rueben raised his hands.

One by one, the others did the same.

They didn't speak as the Masked closed in. There was no point. The fight was over—and the game had changed.

19.

Aftermath

The days after Trial Four dragged by in a haze. Rueben glanced down at his wrist—cleanly wrapped, no longer throbbing, but still foreign somehow.

They'd all been brought back to the room in silence. The beds were freshly made, and a folded set of clothes lay neatly atop each one. In the corner, a barrel fire burned low, its smoke pulled upward by a fan mounted near the ceiling. One by one, they stripped off their blood-soaked clothes and fed them to the flames. The only sounds were the crinkle of fabric and the crackling fire. No one spoke.

The showers ran scalding hot—so hot it felt like their skin might peel away. But they welcomed it. After being soaked to the bone, frozen in rising water, and caked in blood, the heat was a kind of mercy. They didn't scrub. They didn't speak. They just sat beneath the stream and let it run.

After that came sleep. Rueben had slept so deeply he hadn't even disturbed the sheets—odd, considering the nightmares.

Morning arrived with a rush of white.

The door slammed open. A line of doctors filed in, masked and gloved to the elbows, their faces unreadable behind sterile fabric. They looked like surgeons preparing for mass organ transplants. No greetings. No explanations. Just movement.

Rueben sat up slowly, blinking against the harsh overhead lights. The air smelled like antiseptic and something faintly metallic.

One doctor passed by without looking at him, scribbling notes on a clipboard. Another leaned in close, shining a light into his eyes without warning. Rueben flinched.

"Pupil response normal," the doctor murmured, not to Rueben but to the others.

They moved like a hive—coordinated, silent, efficient. Each player was examined in turn. Hazel stiffened when they touched her wrist. Ivy recoiled from the thermometer. Victor didn't move at all. Natalie stared at the ceiling, her expression blank.

Rueben counted them. Five players left. Himself, Hazel, Ivy, Victor, Natalie.

He'd expected fewer. Trial Four had been brutal, but it hadn't claimed anyone. Trinity had perished in Trial Three.

The doctors didn't seem interested in the players' comfort. They poked, prodded, scanned, and scribbled. One held a vial of blood up to the light, inspecting it like wine.

Rueben felt like livestock.

"Vitals stable," someone said.

Another doctor paused at the foot of Rueben's bed, flipping through a thick folder. His gloved fingers hovered over Rueben's name.

"Surprised this one is still alive," he murmured - more to himself than to anyone else.

The words hung in the air, thick and unforgiving.

Rueben didn't respond. He just stared at the doctor's gloved hands, wondering what the doctors would do if he suddenly collapsed. Would they rush to help? Would they even care?

He wasn't sure which answer scared him more.

Across the room, a pair of doctors lingered at Hazel's bedside. Longer than they had with the others.

One of them whispered something Rueben couldn't hear. The other nodded and adjusted Hazel's IV, then checked her vitals again—twice.

Hazel didn't speak. Her eyes flicked toward Rueben for a second, then away.

Rueben frowned.

They hadn't done that with anyone else.

Was something wrong, or were they picking favorites?

The days that followed blurred together.

Rueben spent most of them lying still, watching the light above him flicker on and off. Each flash caused spots to blur across his vision, like ghosts left burned into the ceiling. His wrist had stopped aching. The bandages were changed twice a day. Hazel did it once herself, her hands steady, her eyes unreadable.

No one spoke much. Meals came and went—protein-heavy, flavorless, designed to keep them alive, not satisfied.

Victor kept to himself, pacing the room like a caged animal. Ivy barely left her bed. Natalie stared at the wall, lips moving silently, as if reciting something only she could hear.

Hazel was the only one who moved with any kind of purpose. She cleaned her space, folded her clothes, watched the hallway through the slats in the door. Rueben noticed how she timed the guards' footsteps, how she listened for them to dissappear in a soft echo of retreat.

She was planning something.

Rueben didn't ask. Not yet.

The silence wasn't peace—it was pressure. A held breath. A countdown.

It had been four days since a trial had commenced. They were getting time to heal, and that made Rueben uneasy. How difficult would this next trial be?

Rueben must have drifted off.

One moment he was staring at the ceiling, counting the cracks in the plaster. The next, a hand was on his shoulder.

He flinched. Hazel's face hovered inches from his, her expression unreadable in the low light.

"Come on," she whispered.

The others were asleep—or pretending to be. Rueben sat up slowly, careful not to make noise. His wrist now almost completely painless, just a soft throbbing behind the tight wrap.

Hazel was already at the edge of the room, crouched low, listening. She didn't look back to see if he was following.

He was.

The shower hall was darker than usual, the overhead lights dimmed to a murky amber. Rueben's bare feet made no sound against the cold tile. He attempted to move closer to her and his big toe made a cracking sound. She turned toward him with a smirk on her lips, and pointed to the shower stall with the secret door.

They had taken turns showering in this specific stall, ensuring that noone else found their secret panel.

The air in here was stifling. Warm, humid, and still smelt faintly of the dried blood they had washed off days before.

The tile was cold beneath Rueben's feet, the curtain barely muffling the sounds of the hallway beyond. Every footstep out there could mean exposure.

Hazel crouched beside the drain, her voice a whisper pressed between them.

"They won't expect us to try again."

Rueben blinked. "The control room?"

She nodded. "We already got caught once. That's why they skipped breakfast the morning of the last two trials. They were punishing us."

Rueben remembered the sting of that morning—the hollow ache, the way the others had been confused. They did not even understand why breakfast had been witheld that morning. A pang of guilt stabbing him in the gut. He shifted back to the conversation, a welcome distraction.

"So they think we learned our lesson," he said.

Hazel's mouth twisted into something like a smile. "They think we're scared."

Rueben leaned back against the tile, letting the idea settle.

"If we get in," he murmured, "there might be schematics. Blueprints. Something that shows us how to get back to the drainage system."

Hazel nodded. "Security routes. Maybe even access codes. They use that room to monitor everything."

A pause.

Rueben let himself imagine it—just for a second. The tunnel. The cold water. The way it had felt like a secret.

"We'd need a distraction," he said. "Something to pull the guards."

Hazel's eyes flicked toward the curtain.

"First," she whispered, "we survive the next trial.".

Rueben's jaw tightened.

"Why wait?" he whispered. "What if the next trial is the one that kills us?"

Hazel didn't flinch.

"It might be."

Rueben exhaled sharply, the sound barely louder than the drip of water from the faucet.

"Then we need to move. Tonight. Before they drag us out to the next trial. Before someone doesn't make it back."

Hazel's eyes stayed steady on his.

"We can't," she said. "Not yet."

Rueben shook his head, frustration prickling under his skin.

"Why not?"

Hazel glanced toward the curtain, then back toward the secret passage.

"Because everyone's healed. Or close enough. That means the next trial's coming soon—probably tomorrow. If we move now, it will be too risky. IF we were to get caught again, it would be worse."

Rueben swallowed hard.

"So we wait for them to hurt us again?"

Hazel's voice softened, but didn't waver.

"We wait because we don't have a route. We don't have a distraction. We don't even know if the control room has what we need."

She leaned in slightly.

"We survive the next trial. Then we move. Fast. When they least expect it."

The curtain rustled—then yanked open.

Ivy stepped in, eyebrows raised, voice sharp.

"So what, you two just *think you can slip out* for a midnight stroll? It's not like you can use the front door?"

Rueben blinked. Hazel didn't answer.

Ivy's gaze darted between them, then toward the shower curtain behind her.

"Seriously. Secret tunnel? Magic soap bar? Because unless you've mastered teleportation, your plan's got holes."

Hazel exhaled slowly.

"There's a panel. Behind the shower. It leads to the hallway outside. There is a control room a little ways down the hall, Rueben and I found it one night but didn't know who we could trust."

Ivy's eyes lit up.

"So we use it. All of us. We hit the control room before they drag us to the next trial."

Hazel shook her head.

"We can't. It's too risky right now. Security will be tight as they plan for the next trial."

"What if we brought the others?" Ivy said, her voice rising. "We could overpower whoever's in that room."

Rueben held a finger up to his lips, urging her to quiet down.

"No, we can not involve anyone else," Hazel said sharply. "This has to stay between us."

Ivy's smile faded.

"Why not? They can help!"

Hazel moved to the edge of the curtain and peered around the corner, then looked back to Ivy.

"There are cameras in our room. If everyone heads to the showers at once in the middle of the night, it'll trigger suspicion. We need stealth. Two, maybe three people max. Any more, and we're caught before we even reach the panel."

Ivy's jaw clenched.

"So we pick who's expendable?"

Hazel's voice stayed calm.

"We pick who can move fast. Get in, grab what we need, get out. But not yet. Not until after the next trial. We need a real plan before we start roaming halls, again."

A beat.

Rueben looked at Ivy.

"You in?"

Ivy crossed her arms.

"Fine," she said. "But I don't feel right about leaving the others behind."

Rueben didn't answer.

Hazel did.

"If we get out," she said, "we'll find a way to bring help back."

20.

The Walls Between

They were huddled in the corner, backs pressed to cold concrete, eyes scanning the rows of beds like sentries awaiting a signal. Rueben, Ivy, and Hazel faced the room in silence, watching for movement. None came.

Hazel broke the stillness first, her voice barely a breath.

"I feel like today's the day. I can feel it in my gut."

It had been two days since the shower meeting. Hazel had been the one to wake them, and now she leaned against the wall as if it might hold her together.

Rueben nodded, glancing at the sleeping bodies behind them.

"If it is, we stick together. No matter what. That's the only way we survive."

Ivy's voice trembled, but her eyes stayed dry.

"Guys… I just wanted to say thanks." She swallowed hard. "My daughter's the only reason I'm fighting so hard to get out. She probably won't understand why I never came home. I just hope my mom isn't letting her watch this. It would scar her for life."

She paused, then looked at them with quiet resolve.

"But with us working together, we have a chance. We survived four trials. We can survive one more."

Rueben and Hazel exchanged a glance—something solid passing between them.

They all nodded, then returned to their beds. More rest needed if the trials began today.

Nothing could follow that confession. Nothing needed to be said.

At this point, they understood each other.

Sleep clung to them like fog—thin, uneasy, never quite restful. Rueben stirred first, blinking against the dim light. Hazel shifted in the bed beside him. Ivy remained curled up, her breathing shallow but steady.

The door opened with its usual mechanical groan.

Three Masked entered, their faces blank behind smooth porcelain. They moved with practiced efficiency, setting down trays: gray porridge, a slice of something that might've once been fruit, and lukewarm tea. No one spoke. No one ever did.

The group ate slowly, each bite a ritual. Rueben chewed like he was counting seconds. Hazel barely touched hers. Ivy forced it down, eyes distant.

Victor sat cross-legged on his bunk, eating methodically, like he was trying to make the food last longer than the silence. Natalie didn't eat at all—she just stared at the Masked, her tray untouched, her fingers twitching against her knees.

When the last spoon scraped against the bottom of a bowl, the Masked began to move. They didn't speak. They didn't look at anyone. They simply collected the trays and exited.

The door clicked shut.

Minutes passed.

Then it opened again.

The same three Masked re-entered. No trays. No food. Just silence. They took up positions in the corners of the room—one by the door, one near the bunks, one beside the sinks. Hands folded. Heads slightly bowed.

Hazel's breath caught.

Rueben sat up straighter.

Ivy's eyes flicked toward the nearest figure.

Victor frowned, glancing at Rueben. "They're not supposed to stay," he whispered.

Natalie stood up slowly, her voice low and sharp. "Something's wrong."

The room felt colder.

Then the speaker crackled overhead, its static longer than usual. A voice followed—calm, deliberate, almost gentle.

"CONTESTANTS. REMAIN WHERE YOU ARE. THE FIFTH TRIAL WILL COMMENCE SHORTLY."

A pause. Then:

"TODAY'S CHALLENGE WILL REQUIRE MORE THAN STRENGTH. IT WILL TEST THE PARTS OF YOU YOU'VE TRIED TO KEEP HIDDEN."

The speaker clicked off.

No countdown. No instructions. Just that.

Hazel's hand trembled.

Rueben didn't blink.

Ivy whispered, "They've never said it like that before."

Victor muttered, "What does that even mean?"

Natalie didn't say a word. She was staring at the Masked, her jaw clenched, eyes wide.

They remained still.

The silence stretched.

Hazel began pacing, her arms wrapped around herself. "They're watching us," she whispered. "They're watching how we react. That's part of it. It has to be."

Rueben stood, his jaw tight. "Sit down, Hazel. You're feeding it."

"I'm not feeding anything," she snapped, but she sat anyway—knees bouncing, fingers twitching.

Victor had moved from his bunk. He stood near the wall, arms crossed, eyes locked on the Masked.

"This is conditioning," he muttered. "I've seen it before. You break people by making them wait. No sound, no movement. Just silence. They are trying to make us turn on one another, trying to make us weak."

Hazel glanced at him. "You think that's what they want?"

Victor's voice dropped, almost a growl. "They want us raw. Stripped down. Like meat before the fire. Tender and ready to be roasted."

Natalie hadn't moved. She was staring at the Masked by the door, her eyes glassy. Then, without warning, she stood and crossed the room.

Rueben stepped in front of her. "Don't."

She shoved him. "They're not doing anything! Just standing there like statues. I want to know why!"

Ivy clutched a frayed piece of cloth, something torn from her daughter's blanket. "You'll only make it worse," she said softly.

The Masked didn't flinch.

Rueben caught her arm. "You want to trigger something early? Be my guest."

Natalie yanked free but didn't move again. She just stood there, breathing hard.

Hazel whispered, "This is the trial. Right now. Watching us fall apart."

Then the speaker crackled again.

"CONTESTANTS. PROCEED TO THE TRIAL CHAMBER."

The door opened.

The Masked turned in unison and gestured for them to follow.

No one spoke.

No one resisted.

They filed out in the hall, only to find four more Masked figures waiting to escort them to the next trial.

They were led down long hallways that they had never travelled before.

At the end of the hall was an elevator. The Masked opened it and ushered all of them into the two metal doors.

They seemed to be going down in the facility, but Rueben could not discern how far they had gone with how fast the elevator moved. It came to a halt with a slight bounce in the floor and the doors opened.

They stepped through the threshold—and stopped.

The chamber was massive. Blinding white lights poured from the ceiling, bouncing off metallic surfaces and casting warped reflections across the walls. The air was damp, thick with the scent of rust and something sour—like old sweat and stagnant water.

A grated platform stretched beneath their feet, suspended high above the floor. Below them sprawled a maze of towering metal walls—some smooth, others jagged, all streaked with rust from years of moisture. The scale was overwhelming. It felt endless. Mirrors on the ceiling created an endless void.

Hazel gripped the railing, her knuckles white.

Victor scanned the layout, his jaw clenched.

Natalie stepped closer to the edge, eyes narrowed.

Rueben didn't move. He was listening.

Ivy broke the silence. "This is much bigger than the last trial."

No one answered.

The maze below was quiet. Too quiet.

Then came the sound.

A low creak—metal straining against metal. It echoed through the chamber like a warning.

Hazel flinched. "What was that?"

Rueben turned his head, trying to locate the source.

Another groan. Then a hiss. Then—

SLAM.

A wall dropped, cutting off a corridor.

SLAM. SLAM. SLAM.

Panels crashed down in rapid succession, reshaping the maze with brutal efficiency. Pathways vanished. New ones formed. The sound was deafening—like a thousand steel doors slamming shut. At the same time, other walls were shifting from left to right, creating dead ends where there used to be resolutions.

Natalie stumbled back. "It's changing."

Victor swore under his breath. "They're scrambling it. Right in front of us."

Hazel's voice was barely audible. "They want us disoriented before we even start."

The final wall dropped with a thunderous crack, sending a tremor through the platform.

Then silence.

A staircase descended from the platform, illuminated by a single red light.

No announcement. No countdown.

Just the sound of metal settling into place.

Rueben stepped forward, staring into the maze.

The maze that had been different just moments before.

The silence that followed was thick—like the room itself was holding its breath.

No one spoke.

Hazel's fingers twitched at her sides. Ivy gripped the railing like it might break. Victor's eyes narrowed, calculating. Natalie stood frozen, her mouth slightly open.

Then came the sound again.

A low groan. A hiss. A creak.

SLAM.

Another wall dropped.

SLAM. SLAM.

Panels crashed down in new places—different from before. Corridors vanished. Dead ends formed. The maze twisted itself into something unfamiliar.

Hazel whispered, "It's not done."

Rueben didn't blink.

The maze was shifting, again.

21.

Labyrinth

Rueben took point as the remaining Selected descended the staircase. Each step echoed beneath their feet, the metal groaning like something wounded. His mind was racing, and the grated stairs swayed beneath him—not literally, but enough to make his stomach lurch. He picked up the pace, craving solid ground.

Hazel quickened her steps to keep up, and the rest of the group followed in tight formation. For a moment, they stood in silence, staring into the beast that lay before them.

The passage ahead was narrow, stretching into the distance before fracturing into multiple paths. Every few moments, the walls shifted—extending, retracting, groaning to life like a creature adjusting its spine. The maze felt alive. Not metaphorically. Rueben could feel it watching. Waiting.

"I wonder if there's a pattern we can decipher from the top of the platform," Victor said, his voice clipped, tactical.

"They don't want us to figure that out," Hazel replied, pointing toward the stairs.

Two Masked now stood at the base, blocking the way up. Five more perched along the steps like gargoyles—silent, unmoving, watching.

"So we're going in blind," Natalie murmured. Almost too quiet to hear.

Rueben stepped into the maze first, the metal floor vibrating beneath his boots. The others followed, their footsteps hesitant, eyes darting to the shifting walls. The passage narrowed, then widened, then narrowed again— like the maze couldn't decide what shape it wanted to be.

"We need a system," Rueben said, scanning the ceiling. "The mirrors. If we track the reflections, we can spot dead ends before we hit them."

For a few minutes, it worked.

They came to a fork in the maze.

"There is a deadend to the right," Ivy said and headed to the left.

They moved cautiously, watching the mirrored panels above for signs of blocked paths. Rueben felt a flicker of control—maybe this could work.

The groaning of metal came again, it was almost like clockwork. The maze was shifting every five minutes or so, but the pattern was inconsistent. It felt as if they were walking in circles. For all they knew, this trial was designed to kill all of them.

The wall tilted slightly, making the passage feel like a boa constrictor squeezing in on its prey.

"Move!" Victor shouted as he grabbed Natalie by the wrist and dragged her to the right.

Rueben, Ivy, and Hazel jumped to the left just as the wall came crashing down. Air rushed past.

They paused, dust settling like ash. No one spoke. The silence felt wrong—too deliberate.

Rueben looked across the wall that had just slammed down to block their path. "Are you guys ok over there?"

"We're alive." Victor grunted. "This wall is shorter than the others, we can climb over."

He hoisted himself up on top and reached his hand out to Natalie. They scrambled across the wall and landed softly on the platform next to the others.

The group continued on, a few close calls here and there with walls shifting toward them or falling directly beside them.

They came around a bend in the maze. How long had they been out here? Minutes? Hours? Rueben couldn't tell, he just knew that his legs were burning from all of the walking.

Just then a groan of metal ripped through the air sounding like a cannon.

A pit opened beneath them, sudden and violent. Hazel screamed. Rueben grabbed her arm and yanked her back just in time. Natalie stumbled, Ivy caught her. Victor cursed and slammed a hand against the wall.

"Back! Go left!" Rueben shouted.

They scrambled into a side corridor, breathless, shaken. The maze shifted again—walls slamming down behind them, cutting off the path they'd just taken.

It wasn't just trying to kill them. It was watching. Learning.

They continued down the passageway, each step feeling tighter and tighter as the walls closed in around them. The maze was moving faster now, like a rollercoaster picking up speed after the first drop.

"Any idea where you are going game master?" Victor scorned from the back of the group.

"I have no idea. But if we stop moving then we die," Rueben responded as he turned right down another corridor.

"There has to be a way out of this maze," said Natalie. She was holding her side as she tried to take in deep breaths.

They were all getting winded. They had to have walked a couple of miles at this point, and there was no telling where they were. All of the hallways were beginning to look the same, not that they hadn't before, but everything was beginning to blur together. Rueben was exhausted and wondered when was the last time that he moved this much.

Rueben turned down the sloping corridor, the air cooler now, tinged with something metallic. He didn't know if it was a good sign or just another trick.

Victor's voice cut through the silence. "You sure this isn't just another loop?"

Rueben didn't slow. "No. But it's different. That's something."

"Different doesn't mean better," Hazel muttered. She was close behind him now, her tone sharp but restrained. "We've been running blind for miles. Maybe it's time to stop pretending you know what you're doing."

Rueben clenched his jaw. "I'm not pretending. I'm surviving."

Natalie let out a shaky breath. "I don't think I can keep going. My side—something's wrong."

Ivy moved to support her, but Rueben didn't stop. He couldn't. If he stopped, he'd have to admit he was lost. That he'd been lost since the pit opened.

"We keep moving," he said, more to himself than to them. "We keep moving until something changes."

Hazel's footsteps slowed. "Or until we walk straight into whatever this place is saving for last."

Hazel caught up, her hand brushing Rueben's arm—not grabbing, just grounding.

"Rueben," she said softly. "You need to breathe. We're not going to outrun this thing. Not like this."

He stopped. Just for a second. The corridor was quiet behind them, save for the labored breathing of the others. Natalie had sunk to her knees, Ivy crouched beside her, whispering something Rueben couldn't hear.

Hazel stepped in front of him, eyes steady. "We need a plan. Not just movement. You said it yourself—this place is designed to kill us. So let's stop giving it what it wants."

Rueben opened his mouth to argue, but the floor beneath them shuddered.

A low groan echoed through the corridor, followed by a sharp clang—like metal slamming into place.

Rueben spun around. Ivy and Natalie were gone.

Not vanished—sealed off. A wall had risen between them, smooth and seamless, as if it had always been there.

"No!" Rueben lunged forward, pounding on the metal. "Ivy! Natalie!"

"I'm here!" Ivy's voice came through, muffled but clear. "We're okay. Just—just stay where you are!"

Hazel backed up, scanning the corridor. "Victor?" she called.

A distant reply came, barely audible. "Still here. I think. Not with you, though."

Rueben turned in a slow circle. The corridor had changed again—narrower, darker, colder. He and Hazel were alone now.

The maze had made its move.

22.

Fractured

"We are going to have to keep moving if we want to find one another," the voice echoed over the wall.

"Victor has a point," Natalie responded.

Rueben was breathing heavily. This situation could not have gotten any worse. They were all seperated now and the maze was still moving in the distance. The changes were picking up pace, which meant they needed to as well.

"Just call out every once in awhile. That way we all can at least stay close," Rueben yelled over the walls.

Everyone responded back with understanding and he looked to Hazel. She nodded at him with determination in her eyes.

Hazel and Rueben began to move, their footsteps cautious but steady. Rueben brushed his fingers along the wall as they walked, hoping the rough stone would offer some clue if they passed it again. But the texture changed every few feet—smooth, jagged, damp, dry. Nothing stayed the same long enough to be useful.

"Rueben?" Natalie's voice rang out, distant and muffled.

He paused and yelled back, "We're still moving! Keep calling out!"

Victor's voice followed, each word echoing strangely through the shifting corridors. Rueben tried to track the direction, but the sound bounced unpredictably.

They kept moving, trying to find the rest of the group. They had a better chance of surviving if they all were together.

"RUEBEN!" he heard Ivy scream and he turned just in time to see her and Natalie disappear behind another wall.

"Where are you guys? I just saw you!" Rueben shouted back as he ran to the wall.

He jumped and tried to grab on to something to try and peer over the edge. The wall was pure concrete and there was nothing to hold on to. Rueben slid down the wall wincing in pain as it sliced open his hand leaving a blood stain on the wall.

"We are here!" Natalie responded, directly behind the wall.

Hazel turned to him, her brow furrowed. "That's not possible. We've been walking straight, and they have been in front of us the entire time."

Rueben didn't answer. He was listening—straining to hear anything that made sense. But the maze was alive, grinding and groaning in the distance, its movements subtle but constant. The walls pulsed with change, and the air felt thick, metallic.

They kept moving, trying to locate the others.

The maze moved with them, forcing their paths to change and constantly switching their relative positions to the others.

The maze was making them circle the drain. They were going to go mad in here.

He glanced at the corner ahead and froze. A faint smear of blood marked the stone—his own, from earlier, when he'd scraped his hand trying to climb. They had passed this way before.

"We're not moving," Rueben said, voice cracking. "We're just—circling. We're rats in a fucking experiment. They have us trapped."

Hazel didn't respond. Her grip tightened on his arm, and for a moment, neither of them spoke. The maze shifted again, and the ground beneath them trembled slightly.

Victor's voice called out once more, but it was distorted, warped by the walls. Rueben yelled back, louder this time, more desperate. The echo returned to them, but it didn't sound like his own voice anymore.

Hazel looked up, eyes wide. "Rueben… I think it's starting to mess with us."

He nodded slowly, dread settling in his chest. Movement was supposed to be progress. But here, it was just another illusion.

They sat down at a bend in the corridor, backs against the wall, the maze momentarily quiet. Rueben's breathing had slowed, but his hands still trembled. Hazel watched him, her expression softening.

"I hate this place," he muttered.

Hazel nodded. "It's designed to break us. But it hasn't yet."

Rueben looked at her, really looked—past the grit and exhaustion, past the fear. There was something steady in her gaze, something that hadn't cracked.

"You keep me sane," he said quietly.

Hazel gave a small, sad smile. "You keep me brave."

The silence between them stretched, but it wasn't empty. Rueben reached out, brushing a strand of hair from her face. Hazel leaned into the touch, her eyes closing for just a second.

When she opened them, it was sadness mixed with hesitation.

His breath hitched as he leaned closer, testing the waters.

She didn't retreat and he used that as a sign.

He kissed her.

It wasn't dramatic. It wasn't desperate. It was quiet, like the eye of a storm. A promise made in the stillness. A moment of clarity in chaos.

When they pulled apart, Hazel rested her forehead against his. "Whatever happens next," she whispered, "we don't let this place take that from us."

Rueben nodded, and for a moment, the maze felt far away.

They walked in silence for a while, the maze unusually still. The walls had stopped shifting, or at least slowed enough that Rueben couldn't hear them anymore. It was eerie, but not unwelcome.

Hazel stepped over a crack in the stone floor and muttered, "When this is over, I am never going to an escape room again."

Rueben let out a dry laugh. "Yeah, I think I've had my fill of puzzles for a lifetime. I think it's time for a career change."

She glanced at him. "You were good at them, though. That's why they picked you, right?"

Rueben shrugged. "I used to think solving things made me useful. I only wanted to help others get through the trials. I wanted them to overcome their fears. Now I'm not so sure any of it was a good idea."

Hazel bumped his shoulder gently. "You are usefel. Even here."

He smiled, just barely. "Still not doing escape rooms."

Hazel laughed—an actual laugh, short and real. It echoed softly through the corridor, and for a moment, Rueben felt something close to normal. Like they were just two people walking home after a bad movie.

The sound of cranking metal drew them from the moment. They glanced at one another with dread. The maze was shifting for the first time in what seemed like ages.

Then the scream tore through the air.

Sharp. Human. Close.

Rueben froze. Hazel's jaw stiffened. The maze groaned again, louder this time, and the walls began to shift with renewed violence.

The moment they were having was gone.

Then another scream sliced through the corridor like a blade.

Rueben's heart lurched. Natalie.

He sprinted toward the sound, Hazel right behind him, her boots slapping against the shifting floor. The maze groaned, walls twitching like they were alive, rearranging themselves with a slow, deliberate hunger.

They rounded the corner—and stopped.

The pit was already open.

Natalie lay at the bottom, unmoving, her left arm splayed like a broken doll. Ivy was crouched at the edge, reaching down, her voice hoarse from shouting.

"She's hurt! I can't reach her!"

Rueben dropped down beside her, peering into the abyss. The pit was deeper than it looked—at least fifteen feet. Natalie's face was pale, her mouth moving but no sound coming out.

"Ivy, wait," Rueben said. "I'll lower you down."

Hazel knelt beside them, scanning the walls. "We need something to hold her—rope, cloth—anything."

"There's nothing," Rueben said. "I'll have to use my hands."

Ivy hesitated. "Are you sure?"

"I've got you," he said, voice steady despite the tremor in his chest. "Just trust me."

She nodded, and Rueben wrapped his arms around her waist, slowly lowering her over the edge. His palms were already slick with sweat from the run over. The strain of her weight pulled at his shoulders, his grip tightening.

Ivy's hands were outstretched, reaching for Natalie. Her feet were in Ruebens face as he tried to hold on to her ankles.

Rueben's fingers slipped.

"No—no, I've got you—" he gasped, adjusting his grip.

Ivy contorted her body and tried to grab his hand with hers.

Her eyes were wide, shimmering with fear—but beneath it, something else. Sadness. Resignation.

The movement was fast and sudden, causing Rueben to falter.

His shoulders screamed. Every muscle begged for relief.

"Please," she exhaled as her body slammed back against the wall. "Don't let go."

Rueben's arms burned. His fingers trembled.

"I'm sorry," he said.

And then his grip loosened around her legs.

He reached for her, but was too late.

Ivy fell.

She landed hard beside Natalie, crying out in pain. Rueben leaned over the edge, chest heaving, Hazel frozen beside him.

"Ivy!" Hazel shouted. "Are you okay?"

"I think—my ankle—" Ivy winced. "Natalie's breathing. We're okay. We're okay."

Rueben felt the floor shift beneath him.

The maze groaned again.

Hazel grabbed his arm. "Rueben. Look."

The walls around the pit began to move—slowly, like jaws preparing to close. Panels slid into place, metal grinding against metal.

Rueben shouted down. "You need to climb! Now!"

Ivy tried to stand, dragging Natalie with her. "We're trying!"

The walls crept closer.

Rueben reached down, stretching his arm as far as it would go. "Come on! Just grab my hand!"

Ivy jumped, fingers brushing his—but not catching.

Rueben screamed. "Hazel, help me—!"

Hazel grabbed his other arm, anchoring him as he leaned farther.

Below, Ivy was lifting Natalie, trying to push her upward. Natalie groaned, her body limp.

Then the first wall dropped.

It slammed down beside them, missing by inches. Dust exploded upward. Ivy screamed.

"Try and use the other wall as leverage!" Hazel screamed in desperation.

Rueben reached again. "Ivy!"

She looked up one last time.

Her eyes met his.

Then the second wall fell.

Rueben flinched as the sound hit—wet, final, unforgiving.

Hazel turned away, hand over her mouth.

Rueben didn't move.

He stared into the pit, now half-covered, the edge slick with blood.

A third wall dropped, sealing it completely.

The maze was silent.

Hazel whispered, "They're gone."

Rueben's hands were still outstretched, trembling.

Footsteps echoed down the corridor—fast, heavy, urgent.

Victor rounded the corner, breath ragged, eyes scanning the chaos. He froze when he saw the sealed pit, the blood slicking the edge, Hazel's pale face, Rueben's trembling hands still reaching for nothing.

"What happened?" he asked, voice low, stunned.

Rueben turned slowly, his face hollow. Then something cracked.

"You're too late," he said, barely above a whisper.

Victor stepped forward. "Rueben—"

"Where were you?" Rueben's voice rose, sharp and jagged. "Where the hell were you?!"

Victor blinked, stunned. "I—I heard the scream, I came as fast as I could—"

Rueben surged forward, shoving him. "Fast as you could? They're dead, Victor! Ivy and Natalie are dead!"

Hazel grabbed Rueben's arm, but he shook her off.

"They were right there! I had her—I had Ivy—and then she fell and I couldn't—" His voice broke. "I couldn't hold her."

Victor's face twisted with guilt. "I didn't know—I thought it was farther away—"

Rueben screamed, raw and guttural. "If you'd been here—if you'd just made it in time—they might still be alive!"

The maze groaned again.

Everyone froze.

Then, with a thunderous crash, the walls began to fall—one by one, slamming down around them. Dust exploded into the air. Metal shrieked. The corridor trembled.

And then—silence.

Where the pit had been, where the blood still glistened, the floor shifted. A new passage opened. Wide. Clear. The way out.

No one moved.

Rueben collapsed to his knees, fists pounding the floor. "I let go. I let go."

Hazel knelt beside him, silent.

Victor stood frozen, the exit directly in front of him, the blood at the pit's edge reflecting in his eyes.

No one spoke.

The maze was quiet now, but Rueben's sobs filled the silence.

23.

The Broken Pieces

Rueben wasn't sure how long he sat there after the walls fell. He had just sat there on the ground sobbing.

Hazel and Victor had given him a moment alone and then came back to try and convince him that it was time to leave. But how could they just leave? Ivy had been a part of their group. She had a daughter to get home to. She was supposed to get out.

He'd screamed it at them, voice cracking, tears carving hot lines down his cheeks.

How could he have allowed himself to get emotionally attached to people in the trials?

These games from hell were designed to kill. He knew that. He had obsessed over them. And then he had become one of the Selected. He knew the previous trials inside and out. He had watched several times over, the same trials over and over again. Studying them. Memorizing them.

He had convinced himself that there was a pattern, a way out for everyone if they could all have just worked together. But then Silas was the thorn in his side, and a danger that needed to be eliminated. Silas had been a monster and tricking him was something that Rueben would have to live with forever, but a part of him did not regret it.

Victor had proven to be a nuisance but had been slowly becoming a reliable partner in these devastating consequences. A notable ally.

Then there was Hazel. She was the one who had brought up the fact that more than one person could get out these games alive, and Rueben had believed her. She just had a confidence that no one could ignore. Then when everyone survived trial four, Rueben had real hope.

That hope came crashing down in trial five when not one, but two people had perished in the aftermath. He could have saved them, if only his nerves and adrenaline had not made his hands so damn sweaty.

Ivy's face flashed before his eyes. The look on her face when she knew death was inevitable was enough to break anyone. Rueben could still hear the loud crunch of their bones being disintegrated in a ghastly nature, echoing inside of his brain. Refusing to leave—like a gnat in his skull, buzzing with every breath, every blink.

Finally, after what seemed like an eternity, a hand was on his shoulder.

He looked up into Hazel's eyes.

Her brown eyes were hollow now. His mind raced back a few hours ago when they had shared a moment in the maze, her eyes had shined a little then.

"We should get going," she said softly.

Rueben couldn't get a read on her. She was not showing emotion, save for the clenched fist at her side.

"*Everyone grieves differently,*" Rueben thought to himself.

His legs felt like jelly as he tried to stand. His legs buckled beneath him, trembling like a newborn creature not meant to stand.

A low, deliberate throat-clear broke the silence.

Rueben turned his head slowly. Victor stood a few feet away, arms crossed, his expression unreadable. He hadn't spoken since Ivy fell. Rueben hadn't even realized he was still there.

Hazel didn't look at him. She just straightened, her fist unclenching as she stepped back from Rueben.

Footsteps echoed down the corridor—measured, mechanical. The Masked had arrived.

Four of them, faceless and pristine, as if nothing had happened. As if Ivy and Natalie's blood wasn't still drying somewhere behind them.

One gestured without speaking, a single tilt of the head that meant follow.

Hazel moved first. Victor hesitated, then fell in behind her. Rueben lingered, his legs still trembling, but the cold stare of the Masked was enough to push him forward.

They walked in silence, the sound of their own footsteps swallowed by the sterile halls. No words. No comfort. Just the quiet shuffle of survivors being herded back to their room.

Back to clean up. Back to prepare.

Because the trials weren't over.

The door unlocked with a loud thunk—no ceremony, no softness. Just the sound of inevitability.

Rueben stepped inside first, and the air hit him like a freight train. The room was colder than before. Cleaner. Emptier.

Three beds.

He stopped.

There had been eight. They had not removed beds until now.

Why now?

The Masked hadn't just removed the bodies. They'd erased the evidence. Ivy and Natalie were gone, and so were the spaces they'd occupied. No blood. No belongings. No trace.

Hazel brushed past him, silent. Victor lingered in the doorway, eyes scanning the room like he was trying to find something that wasn't there.

Rueben's throat tightened. The absence was louder than any scream.

He moved toward the shower without a word, stripping off the grime and blood and guilt. The water was too hot, but he didn't care. He wanted it to scald. To punish. To tear the flesh from his body.
Like the hope he tore from Ivy when she fell.

He pressed his palms to the tile, head bowed, and let the sobs come. No one could hear him over the roar of the water. No one could see him unravel.

Natalie's smirk. Ivy's determination. Gone.

He stayed under the spray until his skin turned red and his legs threatened to give out.

Rueben didn't speak as he stepped out of the bathroom, steam curling around his shoulders like smoke from a fire he couldn't put out. His skin was flushed red, his eyes darker than before—hollowed out, like something had been carved from him. Like something sinister was brewing within.

Hazel and Victor stood waiting. Silent. Still.

The curtain hung open behind him, casting a pale glow across the room. Rueben's gaze flicked to Hazel first, then to Victor, then back again. Something in Hazel's posture had changed—less guarded, more resolved. Rueben felt it before she spoke.

"I told him," she said quietly. "About the panel. About the plan."

The words hit harder than the water had. Rueben froze, his breath catching in his throat.

"You what?"

Hazel didn't flinch. "He needed to know."

Rueben stepped forward, towel clenched in his fist. "And I didn't? I thought you said that you didn't want anyone else in on this plan? The less the better right?"

Victor shifted, uncomfortable. "Rueben—"

"No." Rueben's voice cracked. "You don't get to smooth this over."

Hazel's jaw tightened. "I wasn't trying to betray you."

Rueben laughed, bitter and sharp. "Then what do you call it? You made a decision. Without me. Again."

Hazel took a step closer, but Rueben backed away. His chest heaved, the heat from the shower still radiating off him like a warning.

"You think I'm weak," he said. "You think I'm broken."

Hazel's voice softened. "I think you're grieving."

Rueben's eyes burned. "I think you're scared. And you didn't trust me."

Victor looked between them, silent now. Rueben turned toward the wall, fists clenched, trying to breathe through the ache in his ribs.

"Ivy trusted me," he whispered. "And look where that got her. Are you afraid I will let you down too?"

Hazel moved slowly, like approaching a wounded animal. "Rueben, we don't have time for this."

He spun around. "You had time to go behind my back."

Hazel's voice cracked. "Because I thought I was losing you."

That stopped him. Just for a second.

"I thought if I waited, you'd shut down. I thought you would take all the blame. I thought if I didn't act, we'd all die in here."

Rueben stared at her, the fury draining into something colder. "So you decided for me."

Hazel nodded. "I did. And I'm sorry."

Silence stretched between them, thick and suffocating.

Then she added, "But the Masked are distracted. They're cleaning up the other trial. If we're going to move, it has to be now."

Rueben didn't answer. He just looked at the wall where the panel was hidden, the place Ivy had once stood, full of fire. Full of hope.

He didn't forgive. But he stepped forward.

He took a deep breath and tried to release the tension that had built in his shoulders.

"Then we go now," he said looking down at the towel still wrapped around him. "But first, I would like to put some clothes on."

He took his time pulling his clothes on.

This was the only chance they had and he knew it, but something felt wrong.

Something wasn't right.

Hazel didn't speak as Rueben dressed. She stayed near the panel, posture taut, eyes flicking toward the door every few seconds. Victor had moved out of sight— probably sitting on one of the beds behind the dividing wall—but Rueben didn't care where he was. Not right now.

Rueben pulled his shirt over damp skin, fingers fumbling with the fabric. His hands wouldn't stop shaking. Not from the cold. From something deeper. Something wrong.

The silence felt staged. Like the room had been reset for someone else.

He walked around the corner of the showers and glanced at the door. Still locked. Still quiet.

"Why now?" he asked, voice low. "Why would they clean up this fast?"

Hazel looked up, her expression unreadable. "They always clean up really fast, or they make us do it. Silas died in front of everyone. They got us to clean it immediately."

Rueben frowned. "But they didn't clean up after Hank. Not right away."

Hazel shook her head. "We weren't in the room after dinner. We don't know when they cleaned. And Trinity—" she paused, voice tightening, "—they used the drainage system. You saw it. The water carried everything away."

Rueben's stomach turned. He remembered the way the blood had vanished down the grate, the way that he too could have vanished down the system, had it not been for Victor pulling him out of the water.

He felt a pang of guilt at that thought. Here he was not caring whether or not Victor lived or died, when Victor had been the one to save him. Victor was the one showing humanity when it was needed the most.

Hazel stepped closer to the panel, crouching beside it. "They're distracted. That's the point. If they're resetting the maze and prepping for the next trial, they won't be watching us."

Rueben didn't move. His eyes scanned the room again—three beds, no belongings, no Ivy, no Natalie. Just sterile emptiness.

It felt like a purge. Not just of bodies, but of memory.

He walked to the wall, fingers brushing the seam where the panel was hidden. He flashed back to the night he and Hazel had found it. They had hope then. They needed it now more than ever, and Hazel seemed to have it.

Rueben didn't.

Hazel looked up at him. "You ready?"

Rueben didn't answer. He just nodded once, sharp and shallow.

Victor's voice came from behind the wall. "We go quiet. We go fast."

Hazel pulled the panel open. The hallway beyond was open, bright, and smelled like bleach and a moldy mop head. Rueben stared into the opening, heart racing.

Something wasn't right.

He stepped out anyway, heart pounding against the silence.

24.

Control Room

The hallway was too quiet.

Not the kind of quiet that came from absence, but the kind that felt placed. Like someone had scrubbed the air clean and left it hanging, sterile and deliberate. Rueben's boots echoed against the tile, each step swallowed by the silence. No guards. No cameras. No distant hum of machinery. Just bleach and mold and the sound of his own pulse.

Hazel walked ahead, her posture tight, eyes scanning every corner. Victor followed behind, silent as ever.

Rueben stayed in the middle, boxed in by tension and memory.

Something wasn't right.

He'd felt this kind of quiet before—weeks ago, when he and Hazel had stumbled across the control room for the first time. That hallway had been just as empty. Just as still. No guards until after. No resistance until they'd touched something they weren't supposed to.

Rueben's breath caught as the memory flickered: Hazel's hand on the panel, the soft click of the door unlocking, the way the lights inside had blinked on like they'd been waiting. And then—movement. Guards coming down the hall. Too fast. Too coordinated. Like they'd been watching the whole time and just needed a reason to act.

So why now, with them openly out in the hall where they had almost been caught, was there nothing?

No footsteps. No alarms. No voices behind the walls.

Rueben glanced at Victor, who met his gaze for half a second before looking away. Hazel didn't speak. She just kept walking, like momentum was the only thing keeping her from unraveling.

Rueben's fingers brushed the wall as they passed. Cold. Smooth. Too clean.

Something wasn't adding up.

Rueben slowed his steps.

The hallway ahead branched—left, then right, then another right. Identical walls. Identical lights. Identical silence. He frowned. Had they already passed this junction? Or was it just designed to feel like déjà vu?

Hazel didn't hesitate, but Rueben felt the doubt creeping in. They hadn't drawn a map. No paper. No pens. Just memory and instinct. And right now, his instincts were starting to fray.

Victor walked quietly behind them, eyes scanning the ceiling like he expected something to drop. Rueben didn't blame him. The air felt... off. Not stale, exactly. More like the aftermath of a thunderstorm—charged, metallic, faintly bitter. That was ozone. A scent that didn't belong underground.

Rueben's stomach tightened.

They were deep enough in the facility that the layout blurred. No signs. No markings. Just sterile corridors and the faint hum of overhead lights. He tried to recall the turns they'd taken, but the memory felt slippery, like trying to trace footsteps in fog.

Then it came.

A sound. Distant. Sharp.

Not footsteps. Not voices. Something mechanical. A hiss, maybe. Or a door decompressing. Rueben froze mid-step, breath caught in his throat. Hazel stopped too, her hand twitching toward her side—a reflex that was used for holstered weapons. She had nothing. None of them did. That was the point. Stealth over confrontation.

Escape over resistance. A silent agreement between them, something that would change if they were attacked. Rueben would fight for his life, he was done playing by their rules.

Victor turned his head, listening.

The sound didn't repeat. Just that one, brief exhale of pressure. Like the building itself had sighed.

Rueben's pulse thudded in his ears. "Did we take the wrong corridor?" he whispered.

Hazel didn't answer. She just stared ahead, jaw clenched.

Victor looked at Rueben, uncertain. He hadn't been here before. He couldn't know if they were close. Rueben did. And something wasn't adding up.

He glanced back the way they came. The hallway behind them was just as empty. Just as quiet. But now the silence felt watched.

The corridor ended in a wall of brushed steel. No signage. No markings. Just the door.

Hazel stepped forward, eyes scanning the keycard panel. Same as last time—no slot, no keypad. Just a sensor and a ceiling-mounted speaker, faintly humming.

Rueben didn't speak. He just moved beneath the speaker, gaze flicking upward. Hazel was already beside him, crouching slightly, testing the wall for stability.

Victor frowned. "What are you doing?"

Hazel glanced back. "Same way we got in before."

Rueben knelt, lacing his fingers together. Hazel stepped into the makeshift foothold and rose, balancing on his shoulders with practiced ease. Her fingers found the seam in the ceiling tile, pried it loose, and reached into the wiring.

Victor took a step closer. "You've done this before?"

Hazel didn't look down. "Rueben figured it out. Speaker wire reroute. Crude, but it worked."

Rueben braced himself as she crossed the wires— red to green. A faint spark. The panel blinked once, then twice. The door made a faint clicking sound.

Victor stared. "You bypassed a keycard lock with ceiling wires?"

Hazel dropped down, steadying herself. "We were improvising."

Rueben didn't say anything. He just stepped inside.

The control room was dim, colder than the corridor. Monitors lined the far wall, most dark. One flickered— static, then a frozen frame. A hallway. Empty.

Rueben scanned the room, eyes narrowing. No signs of recent use. No coffee cups. No movement. Just silence.

"We're in," he said quietly.

The control room was colder than Rueben remembered. Not just the temperature—something else. Like the air had been vacuum-sealed. No clutter. No signs of recent use. Just silence and the low hum of dormant machinery.

Hazel moved toward the central console without hesitation. Her fingers hovered over the interface, then began typing—quick, precise, almost bored. Rueben watched her work, remembering what the Masked had said during her introduction, back before trial one had begun: FBI cyber division. Five years. Mostly black ops. She hadn't really talked about it much. Rueben had not asked. When the trials had started he did not want to get too close to her, or to anyone.

Victor drifted toward the far wall, scanning the rows of filing cabinets and data terminals. "We're looking for schematics, right? Drainage system?"

Rueben nodded, already rifling through a drawer near the door. Most of the files were maintenance logs— outdated, incomplete. He flipped through them anyway, eyes catching on anything labeled "substructure" or "ventilation."

Hazel didn't speak. She was deep in the system now, bypassing encryption layers like they were speed bumps. Rueben glanced back once, saw the way her eyes flicked across the screen—not searching, just waiting for the system to catch up.

Victor pulled out a dusty binder and dropped it on the nearest desk. "This place is a maze. If there's a way to get back to the chamber from Trial Four, it's not going to be obvious."

Rueben found a rolled blueprint tucked behind a cabinet. He unfurled it across the desk, smoothing the edges. It showed the upper levels—ventilation shafts, stairwells, drainage access points. But nothing matched what they'd seen before. Too clean. Too official.

Hazel's voice cut through the quiet. "Found something."

They turned.

She was standing beside the console, one monitor glowing brighter than the rest. A schematic—layered, complex, and not part of the standard layout. Rueben stepped closer, eyes narrowing.

It showed a corridor—thin, unmarked—branching off from the ventilation system. It bypassed two security checkpoints and ended near the drainage basin. A stairwell connected it to the lower levels, just shy of the chamber they'd found after Trial Four. Farther down the corridor was the small office they had found. The one with Rueben's file. The one where they had fought back and lost.

Victor frowned. "That's not on any of the maps we found in here."

"Not even the original blueprints showed this drainage system," Rueben chimed in.

Hazel didn't look away from the screen. "It was buried in the maintenance logs. Probably used by the Masked. It's not official. It looks as if it was added after the fact."

Rueben studied the schematic. The corridor was hidden behind a false wall in one of the upper vents near where they were now. Narrow. Isolated. Perfect for moving unseen. Purposefully made to get from this room to that one quick and unnoticed. Something bigger was at play here.

Victor glanced at Hazel. "How'd you know to look there?"

Hazel shrugged. "Rueben mentioned the ventilation system last time. It made sense."

Rueben blinked. Had he? Maybe. The memory felt slippery. He nodded anyway.

The room felt smaller now. Like something had shifted.

That is when he saw it.

There on the screen.

The Masked were running down the hall in pairs.

He counted twelve of them before he realized the danger that they were all in was now very real.

"We need to move! Now!" he said briskly.

Hazel didn't ask questions. She was already moving, fingers flying across the console to wipe the screen and shut down the feed. But not before sending the map to print.

Victor was strumming his fingers across the desk, rapping them agressively.

"This damn thing needs to hurry," he murmured.

Finally, the printer pushed the paper out and Victor grabbed it. He handed it to Rueben who folded the blueprint and shoved it into his pocket and headed for the door.

"They're coming from the east corridor," Rueben said, voice clipped. "We need to hit the vent fast."

Hazel nodded. "False wall's two junctions down. We'll have to move fast and quiet."

Victor hesitated. "What if they're already flanking us?"

Rueben didn't stop. "Then we don't get caught. We don't have weapons. We have to vanish."

The hallway outside was still empty, but the silence had changed. It felt thinner now—like sound was pressing against it from the other side. Rueben's heart pounded as they ran, boots hitting tile in rhythm, breath shallow and sharp.

Hazel led them through the first junction, then the second. Rueben scanned every shadow, every corner, expecting movement. But the corridor remained still.

Then Hazel stopped.

"This is it," she said, crouching beside the wall. She pointed up to the vent.

They were going to have to climb up.

Rueben and Hazel helped Victor through first, he was the strongest and could lift them up. Rueben hoisted Hazel up and grunted as she tried to reach for Victor. Then he felt the relief when her feet disappeared into the vent.

Rueben was next, and he was not sure he could jump high enough to grab onto Victor's outstretched hand.

Behind him the hallway lights flickered once.

Then he heard it.

Footsteps. Fast. Heavy. Too close.

Rueben didn't look back. He just jumped and reached for the hand in the ceiling.

His fingers grazed Victor's hand—but not enough. He fell back hard, boots skidding on the tile.

"Damn it," he hissed, breath ragged.

Victor leaned farther out, arm straining. "You've got one more shot. Make it count."

Rueben took three steps back, heart hammering. The hallway lights flickered again—longer this time. A warning.

He ran.

The leap was desperate, wild. His hand caught Victor's wrist, but the momentum sent him swinging, legs kicking against the wall. Victor grunted, trying to anchor himself, Hazel bracing his back from inside the vent.

Rueben's shoulder slammed into the metal edge. Pain flared. He bit down on it.

Victor's grip slipped—then tightened.

"Pull!" Hazel snapped.

Victor roared through clenched teeth, hauling Rueben up inch by inch until Hazel grabbed Rueben's other arm and together they dragged him into the vent.

Rueben collapsed inside, chest heaving, limbs trembling.

Hazel reached back and slammed the vent cover shut. The latch clicked just as the first pair of boots thundered past below.

They froze.

Twelve Masked. Maybe more. Sprinting. Silent.

Rueben pressed a hand over his mouth, Hazel's fingers already on the schematic that had been hanging out of Ruebens pocket, eyes scanning for their next move. Victor didn't speak. He just stared through the slats, watching the last figure disappear down the corridor.

The silence returned—but it was different now. Tense. Fragile.

Rueben exhaled slowly.

They hadn't vanished. Not yet.

But they were ghosts now.

25.

Down the Drain

The vent is barely wide enough for the three of them. Victor is struggling the most with his wide shoulders brushing against the sides of the cold metal.

The air is blasting in the vent and making it cooler than Rueben initially thought which is a good thing, since the body heat the other two are throwing off is enough to keep the penguins warm.

Victor grunted behind him, the sound muffled by the metal walls. Rueben didn't turn—there wasn't room to turn. Every movement had to be calculated, deliberate. One wrong shift and someone's elbow would jab into someone else's ribcage, and then they'd all be stuck in a very awkward game of human Tetris.

Hazel was ahead, moving like she'd memorized the layout. Her boots barely scraped the surface, her breath steady. Rueben wondered if she actually knew the way or if she was just taking the lead in hopes that she would be the one to get us out of here. He didn't know why but she seemed like the type to hold saving their asses over their heads out in the real world.

"I saved our butts, the least you could do is buy me dinner," Rueben could hear it now and see the look of confidence written on her face. He was actually hoping she would let him take her to dinner when they got out of here.

Victor's breathing was getting louder and silently ripped Rueben from his mini fantasy. He sounded close to being panicked and but Rueben could feel the tension radiating off him like static. The man was built for brute force, not stealth missions through glorified air ducts. Rueben could hear the metal groaning under Victor's weight, and every creak felt like a countdown. A silent reminder that they could fall through the ceiling at any moment.

They reached a junction. Hazel paused, crouched low, and held up a hand. Rueben froze. Victor didn't.

The thud of Victor's knee hitting the vent wall echoed like a gunshot.

Rueben's heart stopped. Below them, voices stirred.

"…she said they'd all be dead by now, save for one."

"…boss won't like it if her plan backfires."

Rueben didn't breathe. Hazel didn't move. Victor clenched his jaw so tight Rueben thought he might crack a molar.

The Masked were directly beneath them. Rueben could see the tops of their heads through the slats in the vent cover. One of them was holding a clipboard. Another had a rifle slung casually over his shoulder. They weren't on alert. Not yet.

Hazel shifted, just slightly, and Rueben caught the look she gave him. It wasn't fear. It wasn't reassurance. It was calculation.

What was she planning?

Hazel moved again, crawling forward like the conversation below hadn't just confirmed every suspicion Rueben had been trying to suppress. He followed, because what else was he going to do—turn around and ask Victor to backpedal through a vent that barely tolerated his existence?

Victor muttered something under his breath. Rueben didn't catch it, but the tone was pure venom. He was unraveling. Rueben could feel it in the way Victor's movements got jerkier, less controlled. The vent was too small for that kind of energy.

They reached another junction—this one narrower, older. Hazel didn't hesitate. She turned left.

Rueben paused. "That's not the way to the drainage system."

Hazel didn't look back. "We need something first."

Victor groaned. "We need out. That's what we need."

Hazel's voice was low, clipped. "You want to take down the Masked or just survive them?"

Rueben didn't answer. He followed. Victor cursed and dragged himself after them.

The crawl got worse. The metal was rusted in places, flaking under Rueben's palms. The air grew warmer, heavier. Rueben's knees ached. His back screamed. He was starting to feel like a corpse in a coffin.

They slid down part of the vent as if they were kids at a playground. At the bottom of the incline stood one lone grate.

Hazel didn't hesitate. She twisted her body, braced herself against the vent wall, and drove her boot into the grate. It gave way with a metallic groan, clattering to the floor below.

Rueben winced. "Subtle."

Hazel dropped down without answering. Rueben followed, landing in a crouch. The room was dim, dust-laced, and familiar in a way that made his stomach turn.

The file room. Trial Four. The place where they'd learned just enough to be afraid.

Victor landed last, heavier than the rest. A shelf rattled under the impact.

Hazel was already scanning the room, eyes sharp. Rueben watched her move—efficient, focused, like someone trained to extract intel under pressure.

He remembered something she'd said back in the holding cell. *"In between hacking for the Bureau I took a few classes, trying to get into field work. Behavioral analysis. Mostly domestic threats."*

It had sounded impressive then. It sounded convenient now.

Rueben shook the thought away. Paranoia wasn't going to help them. Hazel had gotten them this far. She'd mapped the vents, timed the patrols, even knew which junctions were sealed. That wasn't villainy. That was training.

Victor wasn't convinced. He was pacing again, jaw tight, eyes flicking toward Hazel every few seconds.

"She's too calm," he muttered.

Rueben stepped between them. "She's ex-FBI. Calm is kind of the point."

Hazel didn't react. She was at a cabinet now, fingers trailing over the labels. Most were empty. Sanitized. But one drawer was still locked.

She crouched, examined the mechanism, then stood and kicked it. The metal shrieked, but the lock gave. Rueben flinched.

Inside: a folder. Thick. Unmarked.

Hazel flipped it open. Rueben caught glimpses—schematics, trial logs, behavioral matrices. Nothing he could make sense of.

Hazel scanned a page, then snapped the folder shut. "This is what we need."

Victor stepped forward. "Need for what?"

Hazel didn't answer. She turned toward the exit.

Rueben hesitated. "You knew this was here."

Hazel glanced back, expression unreadable. "I knew where they'd hide the things they didn't want us to find. It wasn't an accident that I was placed in the trials. I hacked the system, put myself on the Selected list."

Rueben nodded slowly. That tracked. FBI training. Hacking skills. Strategic espionage.

She wasn't surviving. She was dismantling.

"We need one more file in order to take them down, look for anything labeled "Orientation" or "Selection Process". Anything that will tell us how they set up the trials." Hazel said all of this while simultaneously searching in the filing cabinet closest to her.

Rueben's fingers skimmed the edge of a drawer, dust curling up like smoke. The cabinet was older than the others—metal warped, labels faded. He tugged it open. Empty. Again.

Victor kicked a box aside, muttering. "This is a waste of time."

Hazel didn't respond. She was crouched low by the cabinet, scanning labels with surgical precision.

Rueben moved to the next cabinet. The drawers stuck, rusted at the edges. He yanked one open and rifled through the contents—mostly blank forms, shredded memos, a few trial logs stamped with red ink. Nothing useful.

Victor groaned. "We need out. Not intel."

Hazel didn't look up. "You want to survive the Masked or dismantle them?"

Rueben didn't say anything. He just kept searching, while Victor slammed his fist on the desk.

The silence after was thick. Rueben knew Victor was itching to get out of this hell hole.

Hazel stood, crossed to a locked drawer, and knelt. She examined the mechanism, then grabbed a paper clip off the desk and worked quickly and efficiently to pick the lock.

Inside: more folders. Sanitized. But one was sealed in plastic. Hazel pulled it out, flipped it open, scanned the contents, then snapped it shut.

"Not it," she said, voice tight. "Keep looking."

Rueben moved to the far wall. A cabinet half-buried under debris. He cleared it, opened the top drawer. More trial logs. One labeled Trial Six: Emotional Suppression. He skimmed it, heart thudding. The language was clinical. Detached. Like they'd been lab rats.

Victor slammed a drawer shut. "This is pointless."

Hazel turned sharply. "It's not. There's one more file. Without it, we're blind."

Rueben paused. "What's it called?"

Hazel hesitated. Just for a second.

"New Recruit."

Rueben frowned. "That's not a trial name."

Hazel didn't answer. She moved to the next cabinet.

Rueben stared at her for a moment longer. Something in her posture had shifted—tense, coiled. Like she was waiting for something. Listening to something. Rueben was about to ask her what was wrong.

Then—bang.

The door exploded inward.

Three Masked stormed in, weapons raised. A fourth stood guard at the door, blocking escape.

Rueben dove behind a shelf. Victor shouted, lunged at one, but was slammed into the wall. Hazel dropped low, crawling toward the fallen guard.

Gunfire erupted. The room lit up in flashes. A shelf shattered. Rueben grabbed a broken metal rod, swung at a Masked, caught him in the knee. The man stumbled, snarled, didn't fall.

Victor was pinned, arm twisted. Rueben tried to reach him—then a boot caught his ribs, sent him sprawling.

Hazel moved fast. Too fast. She grabbed the fallen guard's pistol, twisted, and fired—point-blank. The shot echoed. Blood sprayed. The Masked dropped.

Rueben froze.

Hazel didn't.

Victor broke free in the confusion, elbowing his captor in the throat. The Masked staggered, dropped his weapon. Rueben scrambled to his feet, ribs screaming, and drove the metal rod into the man's side. He went down hard.

The fourth Masked at the door hesitated—just long enough for Victor to grab the fallen rifle and fire. The shot was messy, but it hit. The man collapsed, twitching.

Silence.

Rueben's breath came in ragged bursts. His hands were shaking. Blood—some of it his—dripped from the rod in his grip.

Hazel stood in the center of the room, gun still raised. Her arms were locked, her shoulders trembling.

Her eyes were wide, unfocused. Not adrenaline. Something else.

Rueben stepped toward her. "Hazel."

She didn't move.

Victor lowered his weapon. "Hazel, it's over."

She turned the gun on them.

Rueben stopped cold.

Her face was pale, lips parted, eyes glassy. She looked like she'd been hollowed out from the inside.

"I didn't want it to be you," she said softly.

Victor raised his hands. "Hazel, what the hell are you talking about?"

Hazel's grip tightened. "You weren't supposed to make it this far. Not both of you."

Rueben's heart dropped. "What do you mean?"

Hazel blinked, like she hadn't heard him. Or like she was hearing something else entirely.

"I built the trials to find a new game master. To isolate the emotionally unstable. To test loyalty under pressure. You were supposed to fracture. You were supposed to choose this."

Rueben felt the room tilt. The words were wrong. It was not making sense.

He remembered the welcome letter. The one he'd read in the holding cell, half-asleep and half-panicked. A line he hadn't understood then:

Solve the riddle and live or take a chance with a guess. The choice is yours.

Good Luck,

H.C. Game Master Assistant

"H.C.… Hazel Carter…. You are the game master's assistant." Rueben said putting the pieces together.

Hazel's eyes met his. "I am. Almost died a few times too, just to find the *one*."

Victor took a step forward. "Hazel, put the gun down."

She didn't.

Instead, she turned toward the cabinet she'd been searching before the fight. Her hand moved fast, yanking open the bottom drawer. She pulled out a folder—thin, sealed in plastic.

She tossed it to Rueben.

He caught it. His name was on the label.

NEW RECRUIT: RUEBEN B.

Hazel's voice cracked. "You were Selected a long time ago. We have been watching you."

Rueben stared at the folder. His hands were still shaking.

Hazel raised the gun again.

"Why?" Rueben asked.

"I'll tell you," she said.

Hazel's voice was low. Controlled. But Rueben could hear the fracture beneath it—like something splintering just behind her ribs.

"You were the anomaly," she said. "Every trial was designed to break you. To push you past the point of reason. But you kept choosing people. You kept choosing hope."

Victor shifted beside him, tense. "That's why you want him?"

Hazel didn't look away. "That's why I need him."

Rueben's grip tightened on the folder. "Need me for what?"

Hazel stepped closer, gun still raised. "The Game Master isn't just a title. It's a role. A burden. You control the trials. You decide who gets tested. Who gets saved."

Rueben's stomach turned. "You want me to become them."

"No," Hazel said. "I want you to end them."

She lowered the gun—just slightly.

"I was supposed to choose the successor. Someone who could see the system from the inside and still reject it. Someone who could rewrite it."

Victor scoffed. "So you put us through hell just to crown Rueben king of the rats?"

Hazel's eyes flicked to him. "I put myself through hell to find someone who wouldn't become a monster."

Rueben looked down at the folder again. His name. His file. His choices.

"I don't want this," he said.

Hazel nodded. "That's why you're the right one."

The silence that followed was thick. Rueben could hear the hum of the fluorescent lights, the distant echo of boots in the hall. But in this room, everything had narrowed to a single point.

Hazel stepped forward, keeping the gun on them.

"You can walk away, but the guards will just kill you." she said. "Or you can finish what I started."

Rueben looked at Victor. At the shattered shelves. At the blood on his hands.

Then he opened the folder.

That is when Hazel began to tell her story.

26.

Hazel's Story

Rueben said nothing while Hazel spoke, just listened in silence

"Three years before the Fifth Reckoning, Paxen Corporation approached me. They didn't recruit me— they selected me. They already had my hacking record, my behavioral analysis scores, my emotional detachment. I was a clean fit. My job was simple: find the perfect candidates. I hacked into federal data logs, scraped psychological profiles, filtered for isolation. No families. No affiliations. No one to notice when they disappeared.

We called them the Selected. But they weren't chosen. They were convenient.

The Trials were already brutal. But Paxen wanted the Fifth Reckoning to be definitive—the hardest yet. A true calibration. A purge disguised as progress.

Paxen isn't just a company. It's a doctrine. The Compliance Initiative was their answer to chaos. They sold world leaders a dream: peace, order, harmony. But the method was fear. They believed if people were afraid enough—afraid of stepping out of line, afraid of being watched, tested, punished—they'd behave. They'd comply. And for a while, it worked.

The first trials were quiet. Controlled. The survivor figured it out. He saw what Paxen was doing and tried to go public. So they removed him. Erased him. The government covered it up as a recruitment ploy, feigning an investigation. You probably saw it on the news.

Five years later, the world slipped back into violence. Paxen returned—rebranded, sharper. They launched a new set of trials, more brutal, more public. They called it a behavioral study. Said it was for science. But it was never about science. It was about control.

They don't want peace. They want predictability. A world where no one questions, no one resists, no one deviates. And they'll burn everything down just to build it.

You weren't chosen at random. Each participant was given clues tailored to their psychological profile— habits, fears, strengths. You were analytical, methodical. We knew you'd dissect the poison in Trial One, not panic. It was designed to keep you alive.

Silas was the only one who deviated. He was supposed to follow his own clue, but he didn't. He trusted you instead. That wasn't in the algorithm.

Silas wasn't chosen to support you. He was chosen to provoke you. We needed someone who would destabilize your emotional core—someone whose presence would force you to choose between vengeance and logic. Rueben, you weren't just another candidate. You were the blueprint. This entire set of trials was built around your psychological profile. Paxen needed someone who could decode their systems, anticipate their logic, and eventually design new ones. Paxen is the funding behind your escape rooms. You weren't being tested. You were being cultivated. Every clue, every scenario, every loss—it was curated to shape you. Not to survive. To become.

I wasn't there to survive. I was there to shape you. My assignment was to push you forward—subtly, strategically. To reinforce your instincts, redirect your doubts, and mold you into what Paxen needed. They called it embedded conditioning. I was supposed to be your mirror. Not too close, not too distant. Just enough to keep you moving in the right direction.

But once the Trials started—once the screens went dark and the control rooms stopped watching—it stopped being theory. It was real. The pain. The fear. The choices. I watched people break. I broke.

That's when the plan changed. I stopped trying to shape you for Paxen. I started trying to protect you from them. And now? I want to burn it to the ground.

I didn't have control at the start. I was briefed, yes—I knew the structure, the outcomes Paxen expected. But I wasn't allowed to interfere. My role was observation. Influence, if necessary. But not intervention.

That changed in Trial Three.

When I went down the slide with Trinity, I knew which one would keep me alive. I helped design that trial. I knew the pit would flood. I knew the panic it would cause. But I also knew something Paxen didn't want anyone to find. There was a room—buried, forgotten, sealed off. I blocked the original exit on purpose. I forced the group to search. And when they found that room… it planted something. Doubt. Defiance. A seed.

That was the first time I broke protocol. Not to save myself. To start unraveling theirs world.

I let people die. I had to. I was being watched—every move, every word, every deviation from protocol. I couldn't stop the Trials. I couldn't pull people out. All I could do was nudge the outcomes—quietly, invisibly.

So I focused on you.

You were resourceful, analytical, unpredictable in ways Paxen couldn't model. If I could keep you alive long enough… maybe you could help me dismantle it from the inside. It wasn't justice. It wasn't mercy. It was math. Sacrifice a few to save many. I hated every second of it.

I woke you when the guards were distracted—during prep, cleanup, zone switches. It wasn't random. I knew their patterns. Paxen gave me access to the control room. I was supposed to report on trial behavior, send updates, keep tabs. That panel was installed for me.

But after Silas died, I stopped sending what they wanted. I started watching for something else. I found the blueprints tucked behind a diagnostics file—routes, drainage systems, blind spots. I memorized the path back to this room. I showed you the panel because I knew you'd need it. Not just to escape, but to return.

You think I was molding you for Paxen. I wasn't. I was molding you for this. For the moment you'd stop surviving and start fighting.

So now you choose.

You either walk out of here and die when the Masked catch up to you—or you stay, and we take this system down from the inside.

If you stay, Paxen gives you what they promised: a position. A seat at the table. They'll crown you the victor, feed the public an AI-generated broadcast of the final trial—make it look like you fought your way through and earned it. You become the face of survival. Humanity gets its hope. Paxen gets its fear. And we get access.

But to make it work, you'll have to kill Victor. Not because he deserves it. Because it keeps up appearances. It seals the narrative. It gives you credibility inside the company. From there, we use their own infrastructure— meetings, data streams, clearance levels—to dismantle them piece by piece.

It's not justice. It's infiltration. And it's the only way we stay alive long enough to burn this down."

27.

The Reckoning

Hazel placed the gun in Rueben's hand like it weighed nothing. But it did. It weighed everything.

Victor didn't flinch. He looked at the weapon, then at Hazel, then at Rueben—his expression unreadable, but his eyes sharp with something Rueben couldn't name.

"So that's how it ends," Victor said, voice dry. "Not with a trial. Not with a broadcast. Just a gun and a girl who was too smart to die early."

Hazel didn't respond. Her silence was a confession.

Victor gave a bitter smile. "You know, statistically speaking, you should've been dead by Round Four. But Paxen loves a miracle. Especially one they can mold."

Rueben's grip tightened around the handle. His pulse was a drumbeat in his ears.

Victor stepped closer, slow and deliberate. "I'm not angry," he said. "Not at you. Not even at her. I get it. We all did what we had to do."

He looked Rueben in the eye. "But if you're going to do this—if you're going to take the seat, play their game, wear their mask—you have to promise me something."

Rueben swallowed. "What?"

Victor's voice dropped. "You take them down. All of them. No matter who gets in the way. Even her."

Hazel's breath caught, but she didn't speak.

Rueben looked at her. Then back at Victor. The man who had fought beside him. Bled beside him. Who was now offering his life like a final act of rebellion.

"I don't want to die," Victor said, almost smiling. "But I'd rather die here than live long enough to become one of them."

Rueben's hand shook.

Victor nodded once. "It's okay."

Rueben raised the gun.

Hazel turned away.

The shot rang out.

A body hit the floor.

About the Author:

Hunter Critt is a novelist whose work explores psychological depth, survival suspense, and the emotional cost of resilience.

With a background in psychology and a passion for emotionally complex storytelling, Hunter blends sociological insight with immersive world-building.

The Fifth Reckoning marks Hunter's debut into independent publishing, where creative freedom and reader connection take center stage.

When not writing, Hunter balances full-time work and academic studies, and finds joy in quiet moments shared with their husband and three mischievous cats.

If you enjoyed this story leave a review and then follow Hunter on social media to get updates on book two in the Paxen Accords.

Instagram Handle is @huntercritt.author